Short & Fun Stories

Vol. 3

Black and White Edition

Large Print

Dorothy May Mercer & Friends

ISBN 13: 978-1-62329-095-5

ISBN 10: 1-62329-095-3

Publisher: Mercer Publications & Ministries, Inc.

Stanwood, Michigan, USA

A Gift for you...

Merry **C**hristmas

Hi there, Reader!

Welcome to the Short & Fun Stories, Vol. 3 anthology, designed for the busy person with a few minutes to escape.

Within these pages are some of the best writers in the business. You will laugh, cry, ponder, and shiver, just like with any great novel. The advantage here is that you will get right to the meat of the action, within minutes, without frills.

Unlike other short story collections, this one is by several different authors, thus the variety is beyond wonderful; it is awesome!

Among the authors are successful published writers with many prize-winning full-length novels and a few brand-new writers starting out.

Following each story, you will find a short bio of the author and an introduction to his/her novels, for your consideration. If you find an author you like, there are easy links to more books by the same writer.

The collection begins with a few Christmas poems and stories and progresses to many delightful selections on a variety of themes and subjects.

We have done our best to see that the contents are acceptable for G (General) and GP (General with parental guidance) readers.

Mercer Publ. & Friends

40 Stories, 19 Authors featured in this collection:

Nancy S. Calumet

Raeanna Davidson

Netty Ejike

Kevin Hayes

Chuck Houghton

Gerald W. Kinsey

Dallas Ford Lincoln

Cherime MacFarlane

Amy Mantravadi

Douglas Maxson

Dorothy May Mercer

A Neighbor

Kathy Nerychel

GeAnn Powers

1st Lt. Joseph Ruff

Gail Sheneman

Wendye Savage

Joe Tilton

E.L. "Luke" Ward

TABLE OF CONTENTS

The Sugar Plum Fairy

By Dallas Ford Lincoln

Chapter 1

Cassie was watching her favorite TV show when a commercial came on reminding shoppers that there were only ten shopping days left until Christmas. Christmas was her very favorite time of the year. Now that she was older, eight years old to be exact, her mom let her help with decorating the house, Christmas tree, and even some of the baking. Gingerbread men were her specialty. She and her parents lived in a very nice neighborhood where all the houses on their street decorated with colored lights and even some animated displays. Cars loaded with sightseers drove up and down their street every night to see the beautiful lighted scenes. Cassie's father always went all-out and the local newspaper even printed a picture of their place a couple of years ago.

Being an only child, Cassie had beautiful clothes and wonderful toys. Mother made sure there were lessons including piano, tennis and even ballet. Her parents were very successful professionals as her father was a lawyer and her mother a child welfare counselor. Though not super rich, financially they were very comfortable. One evening while Cassie was doing here homework she heard her parents talking about something called "the economy" and how bad things were going to be for a lot of people this year. Mom mentioned how her case load had nearly doubled and dad remarked something about there being so many foreclosures and bankruptcies. He said lots of people were losing their jobs and homes in record numbers.

"It's sure not going to be a very nice Christmas for a lot of folks this year," he stated sadly as Cassie walked into the room.

"I don't understand, Daddy. What's a fore...fore...?"

"Foreclosure, Cassie. People borrow money from banks to buy houses, but if they don't repay the loan the banks take their house as payment."

"So why do people quit making their payments? Don't they want to keep their house?"

"Sure they do, honey, but when people lose their jobs or get laid off they simply don't have enough money to pay the bank."

"What will they do when the bank takes their house?'

"Well, some will have to move to another town where they can find work, while others may be able to rent an apartment or smaller house. Unfortunately, some will eventually become homeless."

"Isn't there something we can do to help?"

"I'm afraid the problem is so big we couldn't possibly..."

"But, Daddy," Cassie interrupted, "I've got money in my savings account at the bank. I could give that to help, couldn't I?"

"Cassie, I just learned today that the one remaining factory in town is announcing that they are shutting down for good next week. This means several hundred people who work there, including our neighbors, the Arnolds, are losing their jobs! So you see the few dollars you have would hardly make a dent in the problem. Awfully nice of you to offer, but it wouldn't begin to be enough."

"But Daddy, there must be something someone could do," Cassie protested.

Her parents just looked at one another and sadly shook their heads. Mother went into the kitchen and Dad picked up the newspaper reminding her that it was nearly bedtime and that she shouldn't worry about these kind of "adult" things. Cassie went to her room to get ready for bed, vowing to say her prayers asking for something good to happen—some way to keep the people from losing their homes and jobs. Just before going to sleep she read from her favorite

Christmas story book, "T'was the Night Before Christmas," but only made it as far as. "...visions of sugar plums danced in their heads," and fell fast asleep.

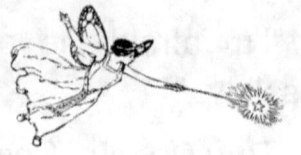

Chapter 2

Well, I don't' know how many of you believe in Santa Claus, elves, or fairy godmothers, but just because you haven't seen things doesn't mean they don't exist. Oh, I know you've heard about the Tooth Fairy. seen pictures in story books and shows and movies about toy soldiers and, my favorite, Tinkerbell.

There also just happens to be another one that a lot of folks don't really know much about. Who might that be, you ask? Why, it is none other than the Sugarplum Fairy. Surly there must be such a spirit because Clemet Moore wrote about it, remember? "...while visions of sugarplums danced in their heads." And a very famous gentlemen, by the name of Tchaikovsky, wrote a ballet called "The Nutcracker" featuring a number called "The Dance of The Sugarplum Fairies!"

One thing is sure...I'll bet you've never even tasted a sugar plum. Neither had I, so I looked it up. Turns out it isn't a plum at all! It is actually an old-fashioned candy made of a combination of figs, dates, cherries, honey, and almonds, rolled into an oval shape then covered with sugar and coconut. I also learned about the Sugarplum Fairies as well. It seems they are usually found in orchards, groves, near streams and flowers and are usually seen at dawn. They like ballet dancing, music, and especially, Christmas! They are irritated by curious, doubting adults. If you should see one, do not approach. And they don't like their pictures taken either, which is why the photos will never turn out or develop, if you should try. Their friends are usually toy soldiers, nut crackers and other fairies.

Chapter 3

Over in Fairyland the Snow Queen was very upset! The major employer in Lakeville had just announced it was closing its doors. This would put hundreds of people out of work just days before Christmas. Something had to be done! Snow Queen sounded the alarm that would summon everyone to an emergency meeting at once. First to arrive were Oberon and Tiana, King and Queen of all the fairies. Next came Fairy Godmother and the Toy Soldiers followed by Tooth Fairy, Tinkerbell, and Elvie, the good elf.

"Where are the rest of the elves, Elvie?" asked the Snow Queen.

"They are all over at Santa's workshop. He said he couldn't spare them 'cause he was already behind with so many requests for toys this year. Sorry!"

"You're right." Snow queen replied. "Santa Claus will certainly need all the help he can get, especially this year."

Snow Queen explained to the hastily assembled group why she had called this emergency meeting.

"I know how busy you all are this time of year and I thank you for coming on such short notice, but I need your help. By now you've all heard about the factory closing in Lakeville. What terrible timing! Now that you are all here I want to come up with a plan to make sure all the children and their families will be able to celebrate Christmas this year."

"But we're not all here, interrupted Elvie. Sugarplum Fairy is missing."

"Well, go see if you can find her. We need everybody. Now, hurry. There's no time to lose. Go, Go, Go!"

I guess if anyone could find her it would be Elvie. He just made it his business to keep track of all the Fairyland residents, both good and bad. The last time he saw her was over by Shea Palace talking with Warren the gate keeper. Shea Palace was the home of grouchy old Gulveig and his little dwarf friend, Bork. Now Elvie was friends with just about everyone in Fairyland you understand, but let's just say he didn't trust Gulveig or Bork very much. He had heard about strange goings on at Shea Palace, which was surrounded by thick walls and looked more like a fortress than a palace. Then there was Warren, the gate keeper whose job it was to keep everyone out. Actually, Elvie didn't know anyone who really wanted to go there and one thing for sure, he didn't! Meanwhile, back at the Snow Queen's meeting Fairy Godmother was speaking.

"There is this little girl named Cassie who wants very much to do something to help the children of families who will be losing their jobs in Lakeville. Her parents are both working, their house is paid for and they are financially okay. She is a very bright young lady but doesn't quite understand how big this problem will become. Yet, she is so determined to help I'm going to do my best to see if I can come up with an idea to assist her."

Tooth Fairy chimed in. "I know Cassie. What a nice young lady! I've been to her house several times while she was sleeping. I want to help, too."

"Well, now that's the spirit, exclaimed the Snow Queen. Oberon? Tiana? You are the king and queen of all the fairies. Surely, you can inspire those in your kingdom to help?"

"We most certainly can," said King Oberon.

"And most certainly will," added Queen Tiana.

Tinkerbell sighed, "I wish Sugarplum Fairy was here. She's so good at this sort of thing."

"I know," said the Snow Queen. "I wonder what's keeping Elvie? Tinkerbell, go see if he could use some help in finding her."

Tinkerbell flew off in a cloud of sparkly fairy dust and headed straight away towards Shea Palace where she spotted Elvie approaching the gate-keeper, Warren.

"Hi, Elvie. Snow Queen sent me to help you find Sugar Plum. Any luck?"

"Hi, Tink. I asked around, but nobody's seen her today. I thought I'd better check with Warren."

"You sure you want to go there?" asked Tinkerbell.

"I don't know where else to look, unless you have an idea."

"Not me," Tinkerbell replied. "I usually try to avoid this place, but I'll go with you, okay?"

Chapter 4

The Sugarplum Fairy sat at the end of the dining table in the huge banquet hall in Shea Palace. She had been invited by Gulveig to come for tea and gingerbread cookies. Not many in Fairyland had ever seen the inside of Shea Palace, let alone been invited to tea. In fact, Warren had strict instructions to never let anyone in without an invitation. So, Sugarplum Fairy was indeed surprised when Gulveig's little dwarf friend, Bork, told her that she was to come to the palace that afternoon, indicating that it was *extremely* important.

8

Bork puffed out his chest and in a deep official voice said to her, "Gulveig says you are to come for high tea this afternoon promptly at four o'clock. He has something important to ask you. And he gets very upset when people are late, so best be on time!"

Bork handed her the written invitation and told her to just show it to Warren at the gate and he would escort her into the palace. Sugarplum Fairy had always been curious to see the inside of Shea Palace; and she assured him that she would be there promptly at four that afternoon. Curious, but also a bit apprehensive, she wondered what this could possibly be about.

Chapter 5

A short while later, Elvie and Tinkerbell timidly walked up to Shea Palace. Warren stood in front of the gate with his arms folded looking very stern and very official in his gatekeeper's uniform.

"What do you two want?" Warren sneered at Elvie and Tinkerbell.

"Well, we were sent to look for Sugarplum Fairy. Have you seen her?" asked Elvie.

"Who wants to know?" came the gruff reply.

Tinkerbell hid behind Elvie's shoulder and managed rather meekly, "Snow Queen sent us to find

Sugarplum. She said if we find her she's to come at once. It's a real emergency!"

"She is here in the palace, but you can't go in. Gulveig said he's not to be disturbed."

"Well, could you just take a message to her that we are waiting outside?" asked Elvie.

"Can't and won't!" replied Warren. "Now go away and I don't care what you tell old Queen *what's-her-name.*"

With that Warren turned and went inside slamming the gate and locking it behind him. Tinkerbell and Elvie just stood there with their mouths open. There was nothing left to do but go back to the others. At least they knew where Sugar Plum was. But, why was she there?

Chapter 6

Inside the dingy old palace Gulveig asked if Sugarplum would care for another gingerbread cookie, as he sat down the plate of cookies. "You must be wondering why I asked you to come to the palace today," he said

"If you don't mind, I have a lot of things to do this time of year. What is it you want?" asked Sugarplum.

Gulveig breathed a deep sign, looked up at the ceiling covered with cobwebs then back at Sugarplum.

"I've got a serious problem and I want your advice."

Sugarplum was astonished! This was not at all what she expected to hear.

Gulveig continued, "This has been a very bad year and I'm not sure I can afford to keep Bork and Warren working here. I know it's Christmas, however I'm going to have to let them go."

"Let them go!" exclaimed Sugarplum. "Go where? What will they do?"

"I don't know, but I have no choice unless you can think of something. They tell me you're quite good at this sort of thing."

"I-I don't know what to say," stammered Sugar Plum.

"Let me explain. This used to be a happy place with lots of parties and fun times. I don't know what happened. Now just look at it. Dark and dreary. And drafty, too. No one wants to come here anymore and my only friends are Bork and Warren. Now I have to tell them the bad news. Some Christmas, huh?"

Sugarplum looked about the dimly lit and musty old room, with dusty, drab curtains covering the windows.

"From what I can see, you've shut everyone one and everything out, including the sunshine."

"Well, I guess I kind of got to feeling like nobody cared about me and then I decided I didn't want to have people come here anymore, so I just told Warren to send everyone away. Please tell me what you think I should do or is it hopeless? I don't even like it here myself anymore."

"Nothing is hopeless at Christmas. Christmas is a time for hope and cheer and even miracles. Hmm…Let me think about this for a minute. I've got an idea. Santa is swamped right now and could use more help. What if you turned this place into a workshop and storage place? It's huge and I'm sure Santa could use the space and extra help."

"Do you really think he would let me? You know I haven't been all that nice to Santa lately. I guess I've been too busy worrying about myself. You might say I've been ignoring him and Christmas. Besides, no one even brought me a present last year!" exclaimed Gulveig.

"Well, see. There you go. Christmas is about giving not getting. It's where the joy comes from. Why, you've just forgotten how it works."

"I guess you're right. Come to think of it, I didn't even give Bork and Warren a gift last year. They didn't complain, though. I really feel bad to have to think of not having them around," he said with a sigh.

"Tell you what," said Sugarplum. "I'm going over to Santa's workshop right now and tell him my idea. Come with me, Gulveig."

"Oh, no, I couldn't do that. I really don't think he likes me."

"Look, if we're going to make this work you've got to change your attitude and get into the spirit, even if you have to make some apologies for your past behavior. Now, come on. There is no time to waste."

Sugar Plum took Gulveig by the hand and off they, went leaving Bork and Warren looking at each other and scratching their heads, wondering what this strange pair was up to.

Chapter 7

Santa was just going out to make sure the reindeer were being fed and cared for. They would need to be well-rested and ready for their big night that was not that far away.

"Ho, Ho, Ho! Sugarplum Fairy. Welcome to Santa's workshop. And...Well bless my soul! Gulveig, too? My, my it's been a while since I've seen you. Come in. Come In."

Sugarplum Fairy wasted no time explaining why they had come. Gulveig made his apologies to Santa, presented him with the offer of help, and the use of Shea Palace for as long as needed. Santa thanked them for coming and said as soon as the reindeer were fed he would come right over to start making plans for the use of the palace. Gulveig hurried back to tell Warren and Bork the good news. Sugarplum Fairy gave Santa a box of her finest sugarplum candies, then rushed back to the Snow Queen's meeting as fast as she could.

"We all need to go to Shea Palace at once," announced Sugarplum nearly out of breath when she reached the others at the meeting.

Quickly, she explained the plan to help Santa to the others and that they were all invited to help. Tooth Fairy questioned the idea of going to Shea Palace and wondered if it would be safe. Sugarplum assured everyone it was and that they would all be amazed when the got there.

Chapter 8

"Well now, exclaimed Santa as the Snow Queen and her followers arrived at the new palace workshop. This is a pleasant surprise. Looks like just about everyone is here."

Snow Queen replied, "Sugarplum Fairy told us all about the plan to expand your operation and we want to help. Just tell us what to do. I know time is short and we are ready to start right now."

That was all Santa needed to hear. Taking a list from his back pocket he began assigning the tasks.

"Since the palace belongs to Gulveig he shall be in charge of building and maintenance. Elvie, you are to oversee the Toy Soldiers who will take over making dolls and trains here in the new workshop. Oberon and Tiana, as King and Queen of the fairies, you and all available fairies will be in charge of gift wrapping the packages. Now let me see...Oh, yes, maybe the most important thing! Warren and Bork, you are to make sure the reindeers are properly fed and exercised daily so they will be ready for Christmas Eve. Who did I leave out?"

"Me, Me, cried Tinkerbell. I want to help, too!"

"I didn't forget about you, Tink. I saved a very special position of gate keeper just for you."

"You--you want me to keep people out?" asked Tinkerbell somewhat disappointed.

"Ho, Ho, Ho," laughed Santa, "On the contrary. I want you to let everyone *in* and give them the grand tour. I want this to become the fun place it once was."

And what a wonderful place it would become! Gaily lit with colored lights. Christmas trees full of shinny ornaments and candy canes; gallons of hot chocolate; and plates heaped with gingerbread cookies for all the workers and visitors alike! Snow Queen was very pleased and thanked Sugarplum Fairy for taking charge. She and Tooth Fairy were invited to the Snow Queen's palace along with Fairy

Godmother to plan the annual "after Christmas" party for Santa to be held as soon as his rounds were completed and he was fully rested.

"Before we do that," said Fairy Godmother, "what about Cassie and the problems in Lakeville?"

"Oh, my goodness!" exclaimed Snow Queen. "I've been so busy I almost forgot. Yes, yes! We must come up with a plan to help Cassie."

As usual, it was Sugarplum Fairy who came up with the idea. Snow Queen proposed that Sugarplum and Tooth Fairy make the trip to visit Cassie in her dreams, (as only fairies know how to do) and explain the plan so plainly that even adults could understand it.

Chapter 9

The next morning Cassie awoke quite rested and full of energy. Joining her parents at the breakfast table she explained the strange dream she had during the night. As she began recalling her dream, her father put down his morning paper and stared at her in amazement. His little eight-year-old daughter was talking about things way beyond her years.

"Cassie," he said, "I don't know where you came up with your ideas, but I'm astounded at the simplicity of it all. I think you just may be on to something. I'm going to make a few phone calls to some people who should hear this. I want you to explain it to them just as you did to me."

First, he called the manager of the factory that was closing. Next the local bank president and then the town's mayor. All agreed to meet at the bank at ten o'clock sharp that morning. Then he called the school to say Cassie would be a little late that day. Cassie liked the idea of skipping school but was more than just a little nervous about speaking in front of such important people. Once all were assembled, coffee and cookies were served (milk for Cassie, of course). Cassie was asked to explain her ideas to them. Nervously she stood, took a deep breath then plunged right in.

"An excellent presentation, Cassie," said the mayor.

"What a bright young lady you are," added the factory manager.

The bank president lowered the glasses on his nose, then looked across the table at the factory manager and asked, "Why exactly are they being forced to close?"

The manager allowed that time had passed them by. Their equipment was old and should have been replaced long ago. With new equipment like other more modern companies they could survive. After all, they were once the leader in the products they produced and their goods were the of the finest quality anywhere.

The bank president looked at Cassie and smiled. "Miss Cassie here thinks we should do something about that. Your company owes us no money and we know your workers are loyal and the finest anywhere. Tell you what: We will lend you the money you need to get the new equipment and technology and help with training your workers. One of our branch offices was forced to close and you can use that building for training as long as you need it at no charge."

Before the manager could respond, the mayor jumped up and offered, "I know you're behind on paying your past due taxes and utility fees. Now we can't forgive those. But I'm sure the town fathers will be glad to wait until you are back up and running to let you pay when you can. That way all your money can go towards training and modern equipment."

The factory manager was overwhelmed and after thanking those present over and over, he immediately rushed back to his office to share the news with his workers. None of them would lose their jobs and this would be a happy Christmas after all.

Chapter 10

Well, this is about where our story ends. What seemed like a hopeless situation actually had a happy ending because people were willing to work together to help others. The factory did prosper and even began to add new workers as the business grew. The local bank made the same offer to several other businesses that had closed and the bank branch building became a permanent training school for all adults wanting to learn new skills. The mayor invited Cassie and her parents to be recognized at a special town meeting and she even got her picture in the local paper!

Over in Fairyland Snow Queen and Fairy Godmother where chatting. Snow Queen smiled and said, "I'm certainly glad we got Sugarplum Fairy to help us with Santa's new workshop and Cassie's problem down there in Lakeville. I'll know who we can count on if anything like this ever happens in the future."

Fairy Godmother sat down her cup and saucer leaned over and patted Snow Queen's hand. "She really is quite good at that sort of thing, you know,"

I wonder, dear readers, who in your life is that "go to" person? On the other hand...Could it be you? Who knows, maybe you are "good at that sort of thing." Give it some thought. You might just end up getting *your* picture in the paper

~~~~~~~~

About the Author—Dallas Ford Lincoln

Dallas Ford Lincoln is the owner and founder of
Lincoln Financial
Services. He studied
marketing at Ferris
State University, and
resides in Lakeview,
Michigan. Now
retired, he spends six
months in Florida, and
enjoys writing.

As seen below, he has an amazing imagination
as witnessed by this display of some–not all–of his
published works. Not pictured here include The
Cemetary Road, Martha's Shawl, and The
Adventures of Fredo and Fife.

For easy access to Mr. Lincoln's amazing array of published works, go here:

Amazon.com : Dallas Ford Lincoln

The Birth of Jesus Christ

Luke 2: 1-20

About this time, Caesar Augustus, the Roman Emperor, decreed that a census should be taken throughout the nation. (This census was taken when Quirinius was governor of Syria.)

Everyone was required to return to his ancestral home for this registration. And because Joseph was a member of the royal line, he had to go to Bethlehem, in Judea, King David's ancient home—journeying there from the Galilean village of Nazareth. He took with him Mary, his fiancée, who was obviously pregnant by this time.

And while they were there, the time came for her baby to be born, and she gave birth to her first child, a son. She wrapped him in a blanket and laid him in a manger, because there was no room for them in the village inn.

That night some shepherds were in the fields outside the village, guarding their flocks of sheep. Suddenly an angel appeared among them, and the landscape shone bright with the glory of the Lord. They were badly frightened, but the angel reassured them.

"Don't be afraid!" he said. "I bring you the most joyful news ever announced, and it is for everyone! The Savior–yes, the Messiah, the Lord–has been born tonight in Bethlehem! How will you recognize him? You will find a baby wrapped in a blanket, lying in a manger!"

Suddenly, the angel was joined by a vast host of others–the armies of heaven–praising God:

"Glory to God in the highest heaven," they sang, "and peace on earth for all those pleasing him."

When this great army of angels had returned again to heaven, the shepherds said to each other, "Come on! Let's go to Bethlehem! Let's see this wonderful thing that has happened, which the Lord has told us about."

They ran to the village and found their way to Mary and Joseph. And there was the baby, lying in the manger. The shepherds told everyone what had happened and what the angel had said to them about this child. All who heard the shepherds' story expressed astonishment, but Mary quietly treasured these things in her heart and often thought about them.

Then the shepherds went back again to their fields and flocks, praising God for the visit of the angels, and because they had seen the child, just as the angel had told them.

Boxes and Bits

By Cherime MacFarlane

Copyright © Cherime MacFarlane 2020

Chapter One

Anya hadn't been in the attic since last year, when she and Stanislaus put the boxes up here. It rubbed her raw as it had every year since they moved to Seattle, moving Christmas to the Protestant's date. The Orthodox calendar worked for her. As the rest of the world went by the other date, so must they. Otherwise, business matters became muddled.

Her family celebrated as they had in Alaska in the privacy of their home. Being Russian Orthodox in a nation of Protestants sometimes became difficult. This year, perhaps more than any other. It would be their first Christmas without Poppa.

Older than Mamma by many years, they all knew, Poppa included, he could well be the first to go. Her stepmother watched him as an eagle watched the salmon coming upstream. Mamma did her best. It wasn't disease or the unforgiving sea which surrounded their Alaskan island home. A train accident took her Poppa and his best friend, Alexis, from their midst.

Anya's eyes filled. She muttered a soft curse in Russian and wiped her eyes. Poppa would tell her all things must end. He had been in God's grace since the day the bear mauled him. When it took his eye and left horrid scars on his back. She must go forward, as he did when it became his turn.

So, she climbed the attic stairs and went in search of the boxes containing the ornaments and bits to decorate the tree. She and Camille, called Mamma by everyone, had divided the decorations the year she moved to Seattle with Stanislaus.

Poppa and Mamma's dedicated manager of the extensive business run out of the Seattle office; Stanislaus couldn't stay on the island. All the years Poppa ran it from the study in the old log home on Bressoff Island had ended. The world moved at a faster pace as the 1800s bowed out and the 20th century began.

She shifted her skirts and sat on the top of a steamer trunk; one Poppa had used. Baby clothes lay in the one she perched on now. Adrianne and Ewing's keepsakes lay tucked away in folds of cloth. There was the christening gown, constructed of muslin using tiny stitches by both Mamma and Helena. Mamma's old friend and lady's maid, the mother of Poppa's friend Alexis Vostvich, had passed years before.

Anya glanced around at the boxes. Stanislaus had labeled them all in his bold handwriting. Fear caused her to put a hand to her chest. So many loved ones gone. Her love, the man she prayed would wait for her, wasn't too much older than she. Anya hoped that meant she would have him for many more years.

This new century hadn't been kind to those living in this world. The war to end all wars, conflicts which had plagued the European continent for most of the last one hundred years, had decimated the youth of all countries involved.

Her younger brother hadn't fought as a soldier. Instead, he worked as an ambulance driver for a hospital in France. She wondered if it might not have been better to be a soldier. As neither fish nor fowl, he'd not done well.

Dmitri was home. He would leave Bressoff Island and move to Seattle. He and his new wife, Marina, must take over the business. Not yet. Stanislaus didn't intend to give up the reins for several more years before retiring to the island. Still, it would happen.

She had come up here with a double purpose; get out the Christmas decorations and go through them to decide who got what. A smile teased the corners of her mouth. And along with what should go to Dmitri and Marina, she must also decide what to give Ewing.

Stanislaus Ewing Rakov, her beloved son, would soon marry the pilot Dmitri had brought to Seattle. Her grandchildren would be Russian, Tlingit, and

Irish. Anya guessed they would be as much a trial to their parents as Ewing had been. It only seemed fair.

The man she loved to distraction had warned her to accept Hattie. As usual, his counsel had been well-founded. Although a few years older than Ewing, Hattie was her son's choice of a wife.

In partnership with Dmitri, they had formed a company and planned to fly people and goods all over southeast Alaska. She worried about the couple choosing to navigate over the rugged peaks and deep waters of Alaska. As it was their lives, she must swallow her fears and pray for their safety.

What would happen when children came? Another question not in her purview to answer. Ewing and Hattie must decide when that time arrived.

Anya rose and took a box from the shelf. An empty one at her side stood ready to receive what she would pass on to Dmitri. A second one waited for Ewing. Being a practical woman, Anya had a third box handy. Someday Adrianne would marry. Rather than wait until that happened, she would get it all over at once.

The first box of ornaments caused the woman to sigh. A bit of fur with a geometric design worked in porcupine quills dangled from a scrap of leather. This was hers and would go up on the tree she put up early for the Protestant guests they would welcome. Their tree must last through January 7th. Therefore, it would not get erected until the last minute.

This bit of fur would hide at the back of the tree. Anya refused to answer questions about it. Her mother, the first Anya who died a few days after her birth, had made it for her while pregnant. One of the few things she had from her mother, Anya valued it highly.

She wrapped it in the square of muslin and placed it to one side on the top of the chest. Another bit she refused to part with came out of hiding. A brass bell strung on a red ribbon; she remembered the day Poppa brought it home for her.

It might well be her first genuine memory of the man who cared for her as tenderly as any mother might. "*Moy sladkiy*," he said as he bowed from the waist and held it out. "*For you moy doch, from the wilds of a place called New York*." His one gray eye shone like a silver coin when he presented the ornament to her. Could she part with it? Perhaps, but not this year.

Chapter Two

The sound of a heavy tread on the attic stairs had her wiping her face, so the man she loved with every ounce of her being wouldn't see her distress. She glanced at the door and grinned when he had to turn his head to the side and ease through the opening.

Stanislaus Rakov, a big man, took up a lot of room. Beside him, her height didn't matter. He fit her to perfection. Even with boots on, the top of her head would tuck under his chin. Picking her up and tossing her on the bed, a feat for anyone but him, always left her breathless.

"So, my love, have you made a start? I expected you to call me up here before this."

The sigh she tried to contain lifted her chest.

He shook his head. "Too many memories." It was a statement. He knew her well.

She held up the bell and gave it a little shake. "It's the first ornament Poppa ever gave me. Not this year. When she marries, I will give it to Adrianne."

"Then you may have custody of it for quite some time. That one isn't ready to give her heart to anyone. She has much of her mother inside. Adventure calls to her. Now that she can drive a car and fly a plane, I think we will see much less of our girl."

"Yes." The little bell went next to the fur disk. "I wish she hadn't learned to fly. That mode of transportation frightens me."

"Heart of my heart, do not allow yourself to descend into fear. They must live, and we must never try to hold them back." His arm went around her waist, and he pulled her tight against him.

"I understand, I do. I remember what I went through getting from the old estate home again." She leaned against him. "The Siberian wilderness almost swallowed my bones. But I had no choice if I wished to see home or see you ever again."

The side of his head rubbed her cheek. "Had I known how difficult the journey; a certain attorney would have lost a few teeth. You were right to keep the entire story from me until we married. I might have killed him in San Diego."

Turning in his arms, she studied her husband's face. "I allowed him to sweep me off into a dream that didn't exist. I said yes to Charles when I could have said no. Tell me, does it bother you to know we are living in sin?"

Stanislaus laughed. "*Moy golubushka*, your first husband is quite dead. The man he became, Mr. Merriman, remains wed to his Chinese bride. They have three children, two daughters and a son."

"You have kept track of him."

"*Golubushka*, when have you ever known me to allow something with the power to cause us great harm to go along untended?"

Anya laughed and let her head rest on his chest. "Never. I suppose I knew you would stay informed of the man's movements, of his life. Poppa trusted you to take care of the business he nurtured and the family. Because of your nature, we will be here until you feel Dmitri is ready to hold his own."

His big hands caressed her back. "True. But I have an ally. Marina is a talented businesswoman and cunning. She will watch Dmitri's back as I did the Count's. She won't give up her business, I understand the girl. Married to Dmitri, she will feel it

30

her duty to help the man. It will be their legacy to their children. Marina will guard it like a mother bear with cubs."

"She will. You are correct. Dmitri will find her a fine helpmate. I want to go home. These people who think they are such high society look down on us. Not only are we Russians and Alaskan, we attend a different church, which bothers them. I'm glad Ewing found Hattie. I shudder to think of what might have happened if he tried to marry one of those who look down their noses at us."

"Well, you have come to terms with having Hattie as a daughter-in-law. Very good. Now, shall I help you go through these bits of memory? You plan to keep these here, I suppose. G*olubushka,* there is no reason to give all away. You should pass a few things on. Our children and your brother will make memories of their own. Give them things which will remind them of Poppa and Mamma, Christmases they remember."

"Yes, please. Give me your help with these boxes and bits. Thank you, love. My heart fills when I think back to the Christmases we all shared. I wish Poppa had been with us longer, but it was good."

"This is one new year I am not ready to ring in. Things in our world are changing too fast. Everyone is in a frenzy to play and have fun. The Count, your poppa, worried about what the next decade would bring. Now, I worry. One cannot play forever, 1920 may go along with little or no change. Eventually, we will all bear the cost."

Her fingers drifted across his cheek. "Let us put that aside for now. Come, love, help me decide what to give to the generation which will one day take up the reins. Christmas, both the Protestant and ours, neither are far off. I need to finish this. What of this one?" She held up a delicate blown glass ball.

Stanislaus reached for a square of muslin to wrap it in. "Ewing should have that one. I remember the look on his face when he saw the candlelight through it. I will put it in his box."

They went through the boxes together. Picking treasures out to pass to their children and grandchildren, who would follow.

The End

If you want to know more of Anya and Stanislaus, read Daughter of the Raven. Click or Go here:

https://www.amazon.com/gp/product/B00F0OCT NM/ref=dbs_a_def_rwt_b

About the Author—Cherime McFarland

Cherime MacFarland has some 65 fabulous novels on Amazon. reasonably priced and available on Kindle and in paper. Some are also available on Audible. For a complete list click on her picture, below, or go here: <u>Amazon.com: Cherime MacFarlane: Books, Biography, Blog, Audiobooks, Kindle</u>

Meet Cherime MacFarlane, Award-Winning, Best-Selling Author. A prolific multi-genre author, she has a broad range of interests that reflect her been there-done-that life. Romance, Historical Fiction, Fantasy, Paranormal, all sorts of characters and plots evolve from a vivid imagination fueled by a voracious appetite for knowledge. Nothing is too esoteric.

As a reporter for the Copper Valley Views, Cherime MacFarlane received a letter of commendation from the Copper River Native Association for fair and balanced reporting.

She was part of the Amazon Best Selling in Anthologies and Holidays (twice), Fantasy Anthologies, Short Stories, and Mystery. Bestselling science-fiction anthology, Legends. Legends was one of the best-selling longest running science-fiction anthologies.

The Other Side of Dusk, historical romance, was a finalist in the McGrath house awards of 2017. Winner of Indielector short story contest.

For a complete list of Cherime's novels go here: Amazon.com: Cherime MacFarlane: Books, Biography, Blog, Audiobooks, Kindle

The Day After Christmas

By Kathy Nerychel

The signs of the holiday are still everywhere:

Christmas cards hung with greetings to share,

Cookies on the counter, bulbs on the tree

Wrapping paper and ribbon from presents opened with glee.

An evergreen wreath still hangs on the door.

Glitter and boxes litter the floor.

Santa and snowman figures on the shelf

All are evidence of a visit from the jolly old elf

Christmas carols are playing in the background.
Familiar songs make a lilting sound.
Under the tree, new pajamas still in the box
Joined by practical gifts like socks.

The smell of vanilla and cinnamon in the kitchen
Joins cups of hot chocolate and gingerbread men.
Fruitcake and peanut brittle round out the sweets.
Everywhere you look there's another treat.

Empty stockings still hang on the fireplace
Until Santa fills them next year, (so be good, just
in case!)
The decor on the mantle shows a wintry scene.
Green and red garlands join lights that gleam.

I'm not ready to put away Christmas cheer
Because I think the warmth should last all year.
We need to find a way to hold Christmas near;
Keep the feeling close with our loved ones dear.

About the Author—Kathy Nerychel

Kathy Nerychel is a retired teacher who has never stopped teaching. She actively mentors more than one group, including the successful Tamarack Writers. Each year she directs their publishing of an anthology collection which includes the best of their weekly gleanings. Kathy spends uncounted hours and weeks collecting, typing, editing, and assembling. Without her patience, guidance, and expertise, that group would not have become one of the most successful in the region, with many published authors..

Without remuneration, Kathy transcribes books for the amazing author, Chuck Houghton whose timeless, first collection *Chuckles with Chuck* has been a best-seller. *Chuck's Chuckwagon of Life*, Dig In, will be out shortly. In both instances, Kathy has typed, formatted, edited, and published the hilarious works from Chuck's handwritten version. (See examples of Chuck's works elsewhere in this edition.)

Is it any wonder that her writers love her?

In addition to her extended family, Kathy enjoys her gardening hobby. Her home is surrounded by blooms seven months of the year. She lives with her husband, Frank, in their beautiful, remodeled, lakefront home near Lakeview, Michigan.

A Letter from Heaven

By Nancy S. Calumet

Excerpt from "Heaven-Sent Love Letters" Between Nancy on Earth and Tom in Heaven, available in paperback.

March 20, 2018

My dear Nancy,

It is great to be able to communicate with you, thanks to our dear friends, James, and Bob who is here for me on this side.

I have been quite busy lately working as a volunteer at a homeless shelter. It may shock you to hear we have homeless people here, but people cross over as they are. They tell me I am doing a great job. Some are cranky, but I get along with them quite well. In fact, they call me Buddy. Some say they don't deserve a roof over their heads, but I say," Yes you do!" I don't try to convince them they are dead; that will come with time. They have mental and emotional hang-ups, but we have psychologists, psychiatrists, and social workers to treat them.

On to my next topic: I have planted some flowers, outside my little house, which bring much color. There is no shoveling snow here, no lawn to mow, and no need to water, to name a few perks.

If it were possible, I would send you a big bouquet for Easter.

I visited your folks recently. They are both fine.

That's all I have for now. I very much look forward to your next letter.

Oh, James reminded me you asked, 'Where is Heaven?' I can't say where it is, but it seems like I took a vacation and ended up on a remote island. Bob says "It is not far away. We share the same space, even though we don't see one another in the physical form."

I see James is getting weary from writing my letter, so I will close for now.

Lots of love, kisses, and hugs,

Yours,

Tom

About the Author—Nancy S. Calumet R.N.

This astonishing collection of real letters, between a widow on Earth and her deceased husband in Heaven, will amaze, thrill, and encourage you as to possibilities of the life to come.

Nancy S. Calumet is the founder of Tri-Angel Ancestry, a family partnership founded in 1992 for teaching Reiki and sending Reiki to those in need. She is a certified Reiki Master Teacher.

Nancy is recognized for her professional skills and accomplishments acquired over forty years in the nursing profession specializing in management, education, and quality assurance.

Widowed in 1990, it was through Reiki and writing poetry she found true emotional healing.

Now retired, she resides in Springfield, Illinois, and welcomes your comments. Her email address is:

nancycalumetrn@gmail.com

Act of Kindness

By A Neighbor

Like many Michiganders, we own a snowblower. In the wintertime, after any significant snowfall, we push it up and down our driveway. Our blower does a credible job on two or three inches of snow, even up to six inches. But woe unto us if more than six inches accumulates.

And so we try to keep up. It is vital to stay ahead during those heavy winter storms. Timing is everything.

Here is the problem: Why is it that you finally get back in the house after sweeping the driveway clean of snow, settled down in front of a cozy fire, when you hear that familiar rumble of the county snowplow service truck? Oh no! The big machine has now deposited all the accumulation at the end of your driveway. It can be four to six feet of the heavy clog—impossible to move with your puny snowblower. Only a hand shovel or a truck can budge the stuff. What to do? Well, nothing, if you live on our street. Just pour yourself a hot chocolate, put your feet up, and relax.

When our lovely neighbor gets home from work, he will be driving his pickup truck with the snowplow attachment. His trusty machine will make short work of the icy mass, which would have taken us days to move.

No charge—nothing asked. Our fantastic neighbor does it to be kind. What a rare and great friend!

My Angel to the Rescue, Again

By Dorothy May Mercer

To my daughters and grand daughters

Hi Girls,

I think that everybody has angels who watch over them. But perhaps, not everyone is as aware of it as I am. My angels have saved me countless times–like today for instance.

I'm sure you are aware of the trouble we have with our lovely, small, feminine ears. They simply do not hold up under so many devices. Having to wear both glasses and hearing aides is quite enough, thank you. Putting on a mask, as well, is straining the system almost beyond capacity. And still we endure, do we not? We make the best of it.

chaos is the new standard.

So today, I was accompanying Dave to the pain doctor. Every six months he gets ten shots into his back to help with the pain. When it was almost time to leave, I put on my Covid mask and went inside the clinic to use the bathroom before I drove us home.

On the way home, I noticed that Dave was speaking softly. I had to ask him to repeat himself several times, as I did not want to miss a single thing he was telling me about his procedure. At last, I did what we deaf people do, I reached up to check my hearing aid.

"Oh my gosh, Dave," I exclaimed, "my hearing aid is gone!"

And so, the search began. We felt all around my collar, the seat, the floor. No luck. We had to get Dave home before I could drive back to the clinic and look for the lost aid. I parked the car in our driveway, so we could do another thorough search. Once inside the house, Dave set my purse down on the counter, as I carefully removed my gloves and coat. We shook out my coat and clothes. No luck. The worst-case scenario was going through our minds. What if this, or that, has happened? My warranty will pay for a replacement, one time, but it is such a hassle in addition to a long wait to have the device manufactured and shipped.

"Before I go, I'll dump everything out of my purse," I said, as I reached for my handbag, "...Oh my gosh!... Here it is!" I cried.

And there was my hearing aid, neatly hung on the edge of my purse in plain sight.

It isn't easy for angels to move things. Imagine those little darlings with their wings whirling tugging that hearing aid from wherever it was hiding and neatly hanging it on the edge of my purse, so I would see it.

This has happened so often in my life that I have named this particular angel "My Lost and Found Angel." It is quite possible that it is a full-time job for her or him.

Ta-ta,

Love,

Mom/Grams

Replies and Comments:

1. "haha Glad you found it!"

2. "Such a charming story. Angels have worked miracles for me many times. I know the exact feeling of searching for a lost item like that.

The one thing I've pretty much given up is earrings that hang. Never fails that I try to take my Covid mask off and it gets caught up in my earring.

Have a great day!"

3. "That is so lucky! Hearing aids are so small it could have fallen anywhere. I really hate having so much pressure on my ears. Mask, glasses, hair, it's all too much.

The Forsaken Monarch The Chronicle of Maud series, vol. 2

By Amy Mantravadi

During the days of Lent 1121, my husband set out for Regensburg to speak with the duke of Bavaria, and the rest of the court went with him. We had passed about a week there in good company. The imperial chancellor in Italy, Philip Ravenna, with whom I had spent so much time a few years earlier, had been brought north to serve in the kingdom of Germany. It was wonderful to have his conversation once again. One day, the two of us and the emperor were all enjoying an afternoon ride in one of the imperial ships down the River Donau, which in Latin is called *Danuvius.* It was a hulk with only a single mast, used solely for river travel. The imperial court had three or four that were towed over land wherever we went.

The three of us were all laying back upon cushions, sipping wine from the Palatinate, when the emperor said, "Let us continue down to Konstanz, for I have business there. I promised the monks of Reichenau that I would visit before the year is out, and I should like to meet with my nephew Frederick and discuss several issues of import."

"Konstanz is in the realm of the Archbishop of Mainz," Chancellor Philip noted.

46

"Konstanz may lie within the archbishopric, but they would be fools to mistake the rule of Adalbert of Mainz for that of their rightful lord," the emperor replied. "A traitor is owed no allegiance."

Perhaps it seems strange that the emperor would call him a traitor. But Archbishop Adalbert of Mainz had been actively opposing him for years and giving no little support to those who rebelled against my husband's will. That is why the emperor said the men of Konstanz ought to support his rule rather than that of Adalbert.

"Is that not the very argument they would use to counter Your Highness?" I asked my husband, sitting up straight. "You still lie under the ban of excommunication, no?"

"Empress Mathilda, you have grown bold since last we met!" said Philip, laughing and spilling a bit of his drink on the deck. He turned his head toward the emperor. "What have you been doing with her? I remember when she was a scared little thing!"

"It's no use, Philip," my husband answered. "There is something of the wild mare about her, but even the wild mare has its uses."

I made no response to this comment, though inside, I was secretly pleased to think of myself in such a manner. I suppose the faintest bit of a smile may have passed over my face as I sank back into the cushion and took another drink of the wine. The ship rocked slightly back and forth as the waves hit it, and the sun was just peeking out from behind the clouds. It was a most pleasant day.

~~~~~~~

The above excerpt is from Amy's sensational novel, *The Forsaken Monarch,* from the series: *The Chronicle of Maud.* It is the second of three novels about the life of the daughter of a 12th C. King of England. In order to cement a political alliance, Princess Maud was betrothed at the tender age of eight to the Emperor of the Germanic nations. As a young girl, she then became the Empress Matilda.

http://ChronicleofMaud.com

Amazon:The Forsaken Monarch

Watch for *The Eternal Queen.* the third volume in the series, due out soon..

Click here for Amy's blog or for information about the novels.

http://amymantravadi.com/

http://ChronicleofMaud.com

Amazon:The Forsaken Monarch

Amazon: The Girl Empress

Twitter: @AmyMantravadi

About the Author-Amy Mantravadi

Amy Mantravadi is a Biblical Scholar, Political Science expert, and History buff with a fantastic memory for detail. Her popular blog, http://amymantravadi.com/,  covers a wide range of subjects.

Amy's education is a Bachelor's in Political Science and Biblical Literature (Taylor University - 2008) and a master's degree in Non-proliferation and International Security (King's College London - 2010)

Although she is still an energetic young lady, her extensive employment highlights have contributed to her unique experiences. Right out of high school, she interned for Congressional Rep. Peter Hoekstra (R-MI) and Sen. Carl Levin (D-MI). In college her journalistic tendencies came out as the Columnist and Opinions Editor for *The Echo* at Taylor University.

Directly out of college her political ambitions led her to Washington D.C. as Assistant to the Director at the Egyptian Press Office in Washington, D.C. (2009-2013). While in the capitol area, she met and married her husband. Now living in their new home in Dayton, OH, Amy cares for their son and continues her prolific writing in her spare time.

George Washington's Wig

By Dallas Ford Lincoln

Let me introduce myself. My name is Winston, and I'll just bet many of you boys and girls reading this story know the name George Washington. He was our very first president. First, I must tell you that I have a very special job in George and Martha Washington's household, but I'm not the only servant in the household. Oh my, there are lots and lots of others. Let me see; there are three or four maids, a laundress, and of course, a large kitchen staff of cooks and helpers. Martha likes to knit, and she has a maid whose only job is to spin wool into yarn. However, I am the General's personal manservant. It's my job to help him dress in the morning, 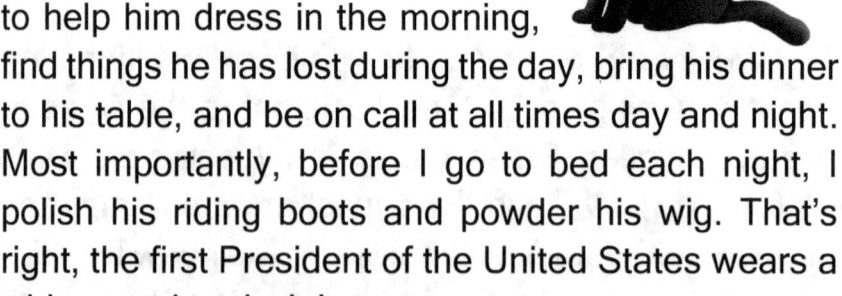 find things he has lost during the day, bring his dinner to his table, and be on call at all times day and night. Most importantly, before I go to bed each night, I polish his riding boots and powder his wig. That's right, the first President of the United States wears a white powdered wig!

I want to let you in on a little secret. Some others live here. The General's wife, Martha, has a cat she's especially fond of named Presley. Presley is supposed to chase the mice that sometimes sneak out of the pantry into the kitchen at night.

Unfortunately, Presley is not terribly fond of her job. She likes to nap in Martha's knitting basket or chase the colorful balls of yarn. To be perfectly honest, she has become very good friends with a little  mouse named Matilda. My goodness, what a strange pair they make! Presley is as black as coal, and Matilda is as white as snow. Presley is a fairly large cat and lots bigger than the wee little Matilda mouse. It seems that we are all taught that cats are the enemies of mice, and mice are a menace to be gotten rid of. And those up in the attic? More about them later. Needless to say, most of the household staff would prefer that Presley behave as a good "mouser" should and get rid of Matilda and the rest of her family, too. Presley is concerned that she will one day be replaced by another cat who actually likes to hunt for mice. To be safe, Presley has warned Matilda to only come into the kitchen at night when everyone is fast asleep.

 Oh, those up in the attic? Overhead in the attic above the kitchen, heard but seldom seen, lives a young family of squirrels. Fortunately, they have not become a bother as the

squirrels never go down into the kitchen or any part of the house, for that matter. They only come and go in and out of the attic through a small hole in the roof. I know this because I've seen them when my chores have taken me outside the house. Winter is just around the corner now, and soon the ground will be frozen. Snow and ice will cover the acorns they have cleverly hidden. Both mamma and pappa squirrel now spend their days running back and forth to the yard below, stuffing their cheeks with the winter's food supply, then running back up into the attic again. They are fun to watch, so we best keep this information to ourselves, okay?

I believe I told you that a very important part of my job has to do with the General's powdered wig. As you might suspect, servants are not supposed to talk about things that happen in the household, but there was an incident that happened recently that involved both Presley, Matilda, and the squirrels in the attic. I'll be happy to share it with you if you promise not to tell anyone. Promise? Now, remember, not a word of this to anyone.

Each night before he goes to bed, I carefully lay out the General's clothing that he is likely to wear the next day. If he is to tend to the plantation, it will be clothing suitable for horseback riding. If he is meeting is with the military, it will be his army uniform, and so forth. General Washington is a very distinguished gentleman who prides himself on his appearance and is frequently asked to give speeches in public.

He would be terribly embarrassed if this story became public. The incident that I'm about to relate concerned a very important meeting he was to attend the following day as the President.

I selected the proper items that he usually wears to such functions and presented them to him for his approval. He agreed with my choices and retired for the evening. I then set about polishing his black leather boots and paying special attention to powdering his one and only wig. When I was satisfied with the results, I put the boots at the foot of his bed and carefully placed his powdered wig atop his chest of drawers on a little stand made for that purpose. That reminds me, I must remember to tell him that his wig will need replacing soon.

Late that night, when the last candle had been extinguished, and the house was still, Presley, the cat, rose from where she had been sleeping under the kitchen table and quietly crept over to the pantry hoping to find her little friend, Matilda mouse. Matilda was wide awake and eagerly listening for the sounds of Presley's soft paws padding across the kitchen floor. In hushed tones, they were soon busy chatting about the day's events, just as old friends often do. Suddenly, their evening's visit was interrupted by a series of rather strange rustling noises overhead in the attic. The sounds became louder and louder and then appeared to be traveling down the wood-paneled wall in the kitchen. Both Presley and Matilda were frightened and held their breaths.

From what I could figure out, Mama squirrel was expecting some little squirrels soon and insisted Papa squirrel go search for something proper for a nest. Not wanting to go outside into the cold, papa squirrel decided to go down into the kitchen that night to look around. He noisily began looking for a way to get downstairs. He scratched here and scratched there looking for a hole in the attic floor. He was about to give up when he discovered a knothole in one of the pine boards that made up the floor. As luck would have it, the opening was just big enough for a squirrel to go through. He stuck his head into the dark hole and began reaching for something to hang on to. He stretched, twisted, and reached as far as he could. Big mistake. The next thing he knew, he was tumbling head over paws down, down, down, hitting the floor with a THUD!

Squirrels often take spills when leaping from branch to branch in trees, and fortunately for Papa squirrel, he was not injured. A little dazed and confused as to where he was, he realized he was not in the kitchen at all but trapped inside the walls. Frantically, he began to scratch at the walls, and this turned out to be the sounds that Presley and Matilda heard. Matilda was very brave for such a small mouse and also curious. She knew exactly how to get behind the kitchen walls. Scurrying back into the pantry, she quickly found her way. A very grateful and embarrassed Papa squirrel followed her back out into the kitchen. Presley was quite amused at all the goings-on and kindly showed Papa squirrel a way back into the attic by using the stairs in the servant's quarters.

Early the following morning, I woke the General and brought him his breakfast tray. When he had finished eating, I returned the tray to the kitchen and then proceeded to help him into his formal attire for the meeting. He took a seat in the overstuffed chair in his bedroom while I brought him his black, shiny leather boots. Then he stood to admire himself in the full-length mirror next to the chair. Satisfied with his appearance, he turned to me and asked for his powdered wig.

As I was so intent on helping him dress, I hadn't paid attention to the fact that the wig was no longer on the little stand on the chest of drawers. I looked on the floor and behind the large chest and even opened the top drawer, but the wig was gone! Well, it was still in the house, sort of. Up in the attic, Papa and Mama squirrel, covered in white powder, were all comfy, curled up in their lovely new nest.

The General was terribly impatient and upset. He kept looking at the time on his pocket watch and reminding me that he could not leave the house without his powdered wig. I searched everywhere. Where could it possibly be? It just seemed a man as important as the President could have more than one wig? It was far too late to consider that. I was truly at a loss and feared for my job.

Presley could not help but overhear all that was going on, what with the shouting and loud voices. She nudged the open pantry door and began whispering for Matilda at the little mousehole in the corner wall there. Moments later, Matilda's little twitchy nose appeared on the other side of the hole. Once she heard about the crisis in the house, she just smiled and told Presley to wait by the servant's stairway, saying she'd be right back. Matilda scampered up to the attic and located the two squirrels who were about to go outside for more acorns. After much persuading and promising a replacement as good or better, she convinced Papa squirrel over Mama's squirrels' strenuous objections to help carry the General's wig back downstairs.

Presley sat patiently waiting at the bottom of the stairs when out popped Papa squirrel carrying the missing item. He immediately dropped it at Presley's feet and scurried back up the stairs. Presley grabbed the "not so powdery" wig and quickly trotted back to the General's bedroom. As I sat in the overstuffed chair, wondering where to look next, Presley walked into the bedroom, proudly laid the wig at my feet, and proceeded to rub against my leg. Oh, my goodness, was I relieved! Let me tell you that evening (and for many more); she was rewarded with her very favorite meal, a fish supper.

I had just finished hurriedly brushing, combing, and powdering the missing wig when the General, or should I say the President, stomped into the room with a red, grumpy face. Pointing a finger at me he yelled, "Winston!" Abruptly, he stopped, smiled, and said, "Oh, I see you found it. Well, don't just stand there, Winston; help me put it on. I have the business of the country to attend to, you know."

Well, this is where my story ends. Presley and Matilda are still very close friends. Matilda usually doesn't have to look far for food when Presley's around. The family of squirrels has grown, a boy and a girl, and they have a very brightly colored nest made from the finest wool yarn from Martha's knitting basket. Me? Oh, I'm still the General's, or is it the President's, manservant. I never know which is it. He now has several powdered wigs. Want to know another little secret? Shhh, I kept the old one!

THE END

Author's Note: People, as well as children, often ask me how I come up with ideas for the stories I write. Here's an example. Some years ago, my young granddaughter, Preslei, was standing next to me. Looking up at the white curly hair on the back of my head, commented, "Hey grandpa, you've got George Washington's hair!" I guess you can tell Preslei is responsible for this one. Thanks, Preslei. DFL

Music to His Ears

By D. Mercer

Dave tested the wire to make sure it was secure. *That's good,* he thought with a sense of satisfaction. *Dorothy will be surprised when she sees what I have done for her, while she's in there talking to Kathy.*

Dorothy had asked him to install a second bird feeder off the upstairs back balcony. He had been putting it off, not that he wouldn't do anything for Dorothy. It was just one of a zillion jobs he had to do before he and she left for a Florida vacation.

Rising from his knees, Dave shoved the pliers into his pocket and dusted the snow off his pants. He pulled back the screen door and reached for the doorknob to open the door, expecting it to swing open. *Holy cow! What tha'? Why won't this thing turn?* Dave jiggled on the doorknob and gave the door a push. *This confounded thing won't turn!* Dave continued turning and shoving in vain, as the stark realization dawned on him: *I have locked myself out. What the heck do I do now?* Dave knocked sharply on the door. He waited. He knocked again. *Surely Dorothy will hear me.* He knocked again, and again.

Dave looked around for a tool. He had no hammer, no board, no rock. Reaching into his pocket he took out the pair of pliers and wrapped on the window. No luck. He peered over the edge of the balcony at the rock garden almost twenty feet below. *No, I don't dare jump. it's too far down. I'd break a leg, or worse.*

By now, the urge to urinate was bothering him. *Well, nobody is looking,* he thought ruefully. *That's a blessing.* Dave whistled softly as he unzipped and took care of that problem.

It was true—the Mercers and the Moores were the only two families living on the dead-end street and the Moore's were away at work and at school. All the other houses had been abandoned for the winter.

For the next half hour, Dave alternately pounded on the door and considered what else he could do. Fortunately, the temperature was a reasonable forty degrees outside, and so he wasn't in any danger of freezing, not right away. It was a little brisk, of course, but this was a sheltered spot and he wore a light-weight jacket. No need for hat or gloves just to do this quick job.

Surely those two women will wrap it up soon. Dorothy would notice her husband was missing, eventually. Then he remembered; Darn it. I told Dorothy I would stay out of her hair while she was entertaining Kathy. She must think I'm still down in my office. Oh great! I'm stuck here.

Dave sighed and leaned up against the railing, trying to get comfortable. There was no place to sit.

It seemed like more than one hour passed when Dave noticed Kathy walking toward her car parked in the driveway. He yelled and waved at her. Kathy noticed him at once and started toward the house. Just then Dorothy opened the balcony door and cried out. A moment of chaos ensued.

Five minutes later, after being rescued, Dave sat rocking in his easy chair, coffee in hand. He managed a wry smile as he watched his wife sitting near him, laughing so hard she could barely talk.

It was music to his ears.

"I'm sooooo sorry!" she managed.

"It's okay," he responded. "It was all worth it, just to see you laugh."

About the Author—Dorothy May Mercer

Amazon.com: Dorothy May Mercer: Books, Biography, Blog, Audiobooks, Kindle

After a long creative life as a combination wife, mother, musician, ordained deacon, music teacher, music director, grandmother, and real estate entrepreneur, Dorothy May Mercer simply did not know how to quit working. She took up a new career as author/publisher & president of Mercer Publications & Ministries, Inc. (www.MercerPublications.com) In the years, since, she has published her own works, including 18 Audible books, 84 titles on Amazon, Lightning Source, Ingram Spark, Lulu, Smashwords, and Barnes and Noble. Also, she has published numerous other books, stories, and poems for her new author friends all over the world, whom she has mentored, advised, and from whom she has learned..

None of this would be possible without the help, support, and hard work of her husband of seventy years who retired after a long successful career. Dave remarks that since he courted her in high school, carrying her books; nothing has changed except the books have gotten heavier.

Among her many awards is the Albert Nelson Marguis Lifetime Achievement Award which is an honor reserved for those who have "demonstrated leadership, excellence and longevity within their respective industries and professions." Dorothy quips that, translated, this award is given to the older, presumed rich, authors, after way too many years being listed in Who's Who, in the hopes they will buy a plaque.

Dorothy's time is full, but she manages to squeeze in a few appearances in person and on radio talk shows, speaking about her book publishing and marketing, answering questions, pitching her books, and teaching others how to do it.

In her post-retirement years, Dorothy immensely enjoys helping and learning from others, so much so, that she has scant time left to write, go boating, or play the piano. If you have questions, or if you just want to meet Dorothy May, good luck finding her. When you do, you will never realize that she has dropped several of her ongoing projects just to focus on you.

It all started January 16, 2011, when Dorothy May published her first full-length book on Amazon, her autobiography.

At the time she thought it was a one-time thing, her last hurrah, but she had so much fun, she just kept on writing.

And so, here we are today.

Thank you for reading SHORT & FUN STORIES, Volume 3

We hope you enjoyed it. Please check our Volumes 1 and 2. The stories are timeless and equally great.

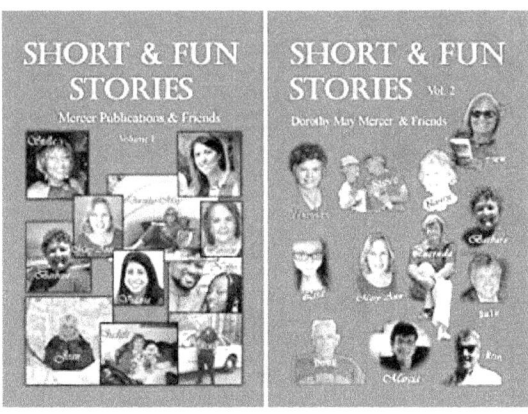

Barn On Fire!

By Chuck Houghton

Uncle Bill Houghton was taking a bath when he heard Aunt Eva screaming, "Billy, the barn is on fire!"

His most crucial farm tool, the tractor, was parked inside. It must be saved! Running faster than he thought possible, he made it to the barn doors, got 'em open, and saved his tractor.

Someone had called the fire department, so he just stood there, watching the barn burn and talking with neighbors.

Aunt Eva stepped up beside him and whispered in his ear, "Bill, remember, you were taking a bath? "Maybe you should go get some clothes on?"

About the Author—Chuck Houghton

Charles Frederick Houghton, golfer, farmer, retired school bus driver, and prolific writer has mastered the rare and difficult art of the short story. As a member of Tamarack Writers' Group, he entertains the members every Thursday with several of his witty writings. His first collection, *Chuckles with Chuck* (Click Here) was published in December, 2018, in paperback and eBook formats,  and his second volume, *Chuck's Chuckwagon of Life*, Dig In, will be out shortly.

Go here for more information: Amazon.com: Chuckle with Chuck eBook : Houghton, Chuck: Kindle Store

Happily married, Chuck lives in Remes, Michigan with his wife Sunshine.

As a founding and faithful member of Tamarack Writers' Group, several of Chuck's hilarious short stories have appeared in their annual anthologies.

<u>People, Poetry, & Prose Anthology Series (2 books) Paperback Edition (amazon.com)</u>

Early Morning Covid19 Visitor

By Dorothy May Mercer

I love the privacy and serenity of my secluded home.

My house is located on a tiny inlet on a small finger of a bigger lake. The surface of the water collects leaves, seeds, weeds, branches, and scum. Moreover, the best sandy, swimming beaches are on the big lake. And so, no one swims in our end.

In the early morning, I fetch pails of water for my little, beachside flower garden, after which I enjoy a moment's relaxation, sipping my cup of coffee, gazing at the beauty, and reflecting on how blessed we are.

We seldom have visitors on this end of the lake. Occasionally a tourist will drift by in his kayak, or a bass fisherman will cast a couple of times and then leave. And so, on Sunday morning, about 7:30 AM, as I approached my little garden, I was surprised to see a white head bobbing around in the middle of my inlet. I had to look twice and clear my eyes to be certain of what I was seeing. Sure enough, as I drew closer, the white head was joined by arms making swimming motions. Not wishing to stare, I gazed at my feet until I arrived on the lakeshore.

Looking up, I saw nothing but a deserted waterfront and shoreline as far as I could see. Was I hallucinating? For a few minutes, I busied myself watering my ferns. All the while, my mind continued puzzling over the incident, conjuring up the images of the white body shining through the rippling water. "Okay, Dorothy," I finally said to myself, "You need to check this out. Suppose the person drowned?" And so, I laid down my watering can and walked out on our dock. "Oh, hello," I said to the young man who was treading water and clinging, underneath the end of the dock, furthest away from me. Clearly, he was hiding. "Are you all right?" I inquired.

"Yes," he sputtered.

"Well...good. I thought you might have drowned," I offered, hoping the man would say more.

"No, I'm fine," he insisted, obviously wishing I would leave.

I turned back to my work and continued watering my flower garden. The man swam back away from the dock and paddled around. Now that I had discovered him, there was no need for him to hide.

At length, he called to me, "Will you bring me a towel?"

"What?" I had to ask. Although I heard him just fine the first time, I couldn't believe my ears.

"Will you bring me a towel?" he repeated.

Stupidly, I asked, "Do you have a towel?"

"No," he called, sounding somewhat desperate.

"Okay, I'll go up to the house," I said and started up the hill. Mind you, going up to the house is not particularly easy for an old lady, but clearly, the man desperately needed a towel.

Inside the house, I chose the most oversized man-sized towel I had and stopped in the kitchen where my husband, Dave, was doing something. "I have a job for you," I announced, "and you won't believe it."

"Huh, what do you need?" he asked amiably.

"I need you to take this towel down to the naked young man who is swimming in our lake."

"Uh, whaaat?"

"You heard me correctly."

"Naked man?" he asked, still unconvinced.

"Yup," I smirked. "Don't you think it would be better if you take it down to him?"

Bless him, Dave took the towel without further convincing and left by the door.

No longer able to contain it, I started laughing steadily for five minutes, followed by another five minutes of periodic outbursts, holding my sides.

And so, my first Covid19 visitor had the audacity to appear unannounced without a mask, or anything else, actually.

Grin and Bare It

By Chuck Houghton

I waved at Dick and Marsha Pant playing Hole Two on the Links of Edmore Sunday afternoon, fondly remembering my school bus driving days. Because of the Pant children's work schedules, the grandchildren got on and off at Grandpa and Grandma Pant's house.

Why did I bring this up? Because the bus stop just before the "Pant's" was the "Buckle's." Once in a great while, none of the Pant's kids rode the bus. If that did happen, some of the kids on my bus would yell out, "We got Buckles, but no Pants," and everyone would laugh.

CD—Compact Disk—or DVD?

By Dorothy May Mercer

Excerpt from How to Get an Audible Version *of Your Book, 2nd Edition*

© 2020 Dorothy May Mercer

As you may know, I have written a dozen or more novels. They are all available in three versions, print, eBook, and Audible formats. I thought it would be nice to have them on CD as well, to be sold to libraries and in retail outlets such as WalMart. However, Audible does not make a CD. They only market the online digital recordings in MP3 format for computer and Bluetooth players. And so, if you want to manufacture a CD, you must give Audible a non-exclusive contract. Such a contract allows Audible to place your Audible recording for sale on Audible, iTunes, and Amazon and pay you 25% of sales. Conversely, a non-exclusive contract will enable you to sell your Audible book in other places and to manufacture a CD if you want.

As a matter of fact, I tried doing that with one of my novels. After creating an Audible version of the book and putting it on a non-exclusive contract with Audible, I tried to manufacture and market my audiobooks myself. It's a long story. Indeed, I learned to make the discs but failed at marketing them. For your edification, entertainment, and amusement, here is the story:

I soon discovered that CDs do not carry enough minutes to hold my novel. The maximum is eighty minutes of sound. My novel was seven and a half hours, or 450 minutes, meaning it would require six CDs to record. If you have ever looked at audio books in a public library, you will see what I mean. And so, I looked into using DVDs instead. One DVD would hold my entire novel. And so, I invested in 100 writable DVD discs, the necessary containers, and all the paraphernalia and software required to make the colorful labels and covers.

My anticipation knew no bounds as I waited for all this stuff to be delivered. I tore open the packages when they arrived, happy as a field mouse in a harvest bin. Soon, I was busy reading instructions and installing software on my computer. The hours and days flew by as I immersed myself in my favorite activity–creating.

As you may have guessed, one thing called for another as expenses mounted. But the happy day came when I completed my first DVD, shrink-wrapped it with a copy of the print book, took it to my local retail outlet, and placed it in the book sales display.

Not every endeavor is destined for success, as you know. Perhaps I should have considered that not all CD players will also play a DVD. One needs a DVD player or a combination player.

Months later, the book plus DVD was gathering dust, still awaiting its first sale. Indeed, I needed a better marketing plan.

There is a company that markets Audible books to libraries. And so, I applied to them. But they needed a list of my "catalog" of "dozens" of Audible CDs and DVDs, as well as a much more extensive inventory. They never responded. Clearly, one DVD was not enough. I would need a large library of DVDs of all my novels for any hope of placing them with that marketing company.

At that time, I had no further marketing plan and so, I moved on.

How to Fight a Bad Review

By Dorothy May Mercer

Dear Author Friend,

You asked for my advice regarding what to do about a particularly bad Amazon review. I read the one-star review which you received for My Story. You are quite right; this review is persuasive and devastating. The writer makes it clear that she has read the book and goes on to explain in detail exactly what she found wrong. It will do incredible damage, not only to this book but to your reputation, and ultimately hurt the sales of your other books, as well.

For the author, it is emotionally painful and can be depressing to receive a bad review. It helps to know that every successful author receives them. The more successful the book, the more hate will result. And so, it helps to know you are in good company. The question is, what are you going to do about it, quit or pick yourself up and go on?

If the latter choice, then it is imperative that you forgive the author of the bad review, pray for that person, and learn as much as you can from the content of the review. Maybe there are some valid points. If not, then it is best to rejoice and put it behind you as soon as possible.

The only way to destroy all the reviews is to delete the book. It may be necessary to take this book off the market (more later), but before you do that, there are a few things you can quickly try if you wish to do so.

1. Amazon allows you to sort between "Most recent" and "Top rated." I have sorted your book's reviews by "Most recent," thus allowing a different five-star review to be first, dropping the one-star review to second place. If you can get some friends to post new reviews, that could lower the lousy review further down. You could contact people who have already posted and ask them to read the bad review and update their review accordingly. (Only the writer who posted any review can delete or change it.) Meanwhile, you can go into the sales page every day and sort your reviews by "Most Recent."

2. Amazon allows you to check "Helpful" or "Report abuse." I checked all the Helpful ones for you. But you and your friends can do this every day, as well.

3. If you have ever received an "editorial" review—even if the publication was tiny or on someone's blog—you can enter that into the sales page as an "editorial" review. (The wordier, and longer, the better.) You can also edit out any negative part, so long as you place an ellipsis in the deleted space.

This editorial review will appear after the opening description and will be the first thing an Amazon customer notices.

The way to do this is to go to your author page (authorcentral.amazon.com). I googled the question and found these items online:

[Follow these] Steps for Adding Your Editorial Review to Amazon.

Log in to Author Central.

Click on the Books tab at the top of the page.

Go to your Book Page.

Click on the title of the book you want to edit.

Choose "Under Editorial Reviews" and click "add" review.

Here is a link to another article online: How to add editorial reviews to your book's amazon page - Old Mate Media

4. Finally, as a last resort, you can take the book, along with all its reviews, off Amazon, rewrite, and publish with a new ISBN number, cover and description

A. Go to your account at kdp.amazon.com. Locate the book. To the far right of the print book, hover over the ellipsis (three tiny dots). Select "unpublish print book." Repeat this process with the ebook.

B. Rewrite your book, taking care to refute the claims made in the bad review without actually identifying that review. As much as possible, fix any valid areas which were criticized.

C. Rename this new version, such as *My Story, Revised.*

D. Design a new cover.

E. Use a new ISBN. In your new description, refer to the "new-found" evidence, etc.

F. Publish.

Good luck,

Dorothy

GO FOR IT !

GOOD LUCK !

Limerick

By Raeanna Davidson

There once was a cow

Who learned how to bow.

His color was yellow

Because he liked jello.

Some folks looked and said,

"Bow now, clown cow!"

About the Author—Raeanna Davidson

The author is an adopted daughter, and member of a big family. She writes and draws illustrations every day, and especially loves writing stories for her nieces and nephews and all the children in the world, to teach them how to count and read.

She is very active in her church and in various local charity projects. Raeanna is member of the Tamarack Writers' of Lakeview, Michigan and has several articles and poems published in their 2019 and 2020 Anthologies.

For links, please go here: Amazon.com : Tamarack Writers

They Are a-Changing

By Luke Ward

I guess it really started with the surveillance cameras they put in at all the workstations. For a while after the installation, the foremen were coming around more often, confronting us on every little thing. It seemed a little vaudeville honestly they probably just wanted to let us know they were watching. That first shakeup was easy enough to shrug off, I think. But the big change was the *speakers*. After that, the foremen didn't come around at all anymore.

I didn't mind so much after a while, getting all my instructions (and occasionally being bawled out) over intercom. Talking to a speaker with a little lens over it on a mobile stand, and having it order me around, felt a bit demeaning at first, sure. But I've never had any particular vendetta against innovation, so I tried to find the silver lining. As time went by, I convinced myself my foreman seemed less surly when there was no face to go with the voice. It was a good look for him if truth be told.

Naturally, it was just about the time I really got used to the new workflow when something else changed. One day the voice over the speaker was no longer my foreman's voice. It wasn't anyone's voice in particular, in fact. Yes, I could tell right away from the stunted, fits-and-starts pacing and the strange emphasis that it was software I was speaking to. I had to admit that was a bit puzzling. We weren't really told how things had been reorganized, after all... or even that they were going to *be* reorganized in the first place. To this day, I'm not sure what my foreman does anymore, or whether he's even still with the company. There was just a voice simulator giving me order all of a sudden—me and everyone else on the production floor. He asked that we call him "Jeff."

Jeff seemed a little off from the start, to be honest. At first, I just thought his voice recognition programming was sluggish. But it was more than that. His answers weren't just slow in coming; they felt reluctant. I started to get the feeling he was a bit...uh...preoccupied. Indecisive, even. And it showed in the monthly production reports. R&A's went up, yield went down. And when the numbers came in, they seemed to take some toll on Jeff, too. At times it almost felt we had to coax him just to lead us.

Things improved a bit later on, though. I came into work and was greeted by a new computer voice: "Sarah". In the back of my mind I wondered what became of Jeff, but I learned soon enough he was still around. Sarah put me on a cross-training regimen, at which point I discovered a whole ensemble of new voices had simply been installed to take the pressure off Jeff; and they each juggled just a few machine centers. It seemed like a smart move, and I thought for sure things would be looking up from then on.

But that was when things began to get strange. Within days the artificial voices all seemed to start coming down with Jeff's malaise. For a week or so, they were just sort of sulky and reticent. And when they thought we were too busy to notice, they'd congregate in small groups - two or three little speaker sets huddled in a corner murmuring. It was immediately clear something was bothering them. But we didn't ask... and they certainly didn't volunteer anything. When, after perhaps a month of this, they kind of opened up, it proved to be even more uncomfortable. I'd be working along, and suddenly Sarah or Jeff or Milford would corner me with difficult questions. What did I suppose was the meaning of life? How did I cope with the loss of loved ones? How did it feel to have one's circuits overheat and fuse? It was always something melancholy like that. I would always fumble for the most reassuring answers I could. But it never did any good.

Well, a man can only take so much of that atmosphere. I gave them my two weeks and got out of there. I'm no psychiatrist, after all. Fortunately, I found a decent job in livestock drafting, and I've been much happier there. But every so often, I can't help wondering whatever became of Jeff, and Sarah, and the lot. I hope somehow they're doing better...

About the Author—Luke Ward

[Note: A reviewer had this to say about Luke: "Luke has a great imagination, knows how to hold the reader in suspense and then "Bang" he grabs you. I see a long and diverse career for this gentleman."]

Luke Ward is a serious writer who, like many artists, still keeps his day job. Nevertheless, he spends every spare moment writing books, and marketing them. He appears frequently at book fairs, book signings and author events in Western Michigan. Luke is active in the Tamarack Writers' Group and seeks their advice on his latest writing endeavors. His works have been published in the Tamarack Writers' 2020 Anthology. Watch for many future books from Luke's fertile imagination.

He is currently working on the third book in his "Horus Templar - Public Defender" series: "Horus Templar and the Case of the Draft-Dodging Drone". Like his previous books, it takes place in a medieval fantasy setting. There will be adventure, legal drama, and most certainly a few laughs. Luke's stated goal is to finish writing the book by the end of 2021.

Please click on any cover to go directly to the Amazon page or do a search for E.L. Ward (Not to be confused with another author by the name of Luke Ward).

Not So Celebrated

By E. L. Ward

[Note: Luke Ward writes with the penname, E.L. Ward. His self-deprecating author's bio is on Amazon. It is so hilarious, we asked him for the privilege of reprinting it here.]

E.L. Ward is the celebrated author of one title, including The Chocolate Prophecy. New York Times Bestseller, the Pulitzer Prize, the PEN/Faulkner Award for Fiction, a Tony, Grammy, and Oscar, the Nobel Peace Prize, Best in Show, Blue Ribbon, Student of the Month, and World's Best Dad *are all among the accolades he wouldn't mind achieving one day*. He has had his picture in the newspaper once.

Ward lives in Michigan, basically.

Prior to his vaunted career as a starving artist, Ward distinguished himself in education, graduating 13th in his class, and receiving cute little awards for Media Production and Industrial Technology at one point. He went on to attain a phony-baloney Bachelor of Art in Communications, Film and Video Concentration, from Grand Valley State University. Their film school actually requires secondary enrollment, so to attain such a degree was way, way harder than it even sounds, which is worth noting.

Even after such wuthering heights, there was still nowhere for a man like Ward to go but up. He spent literally hours battling to claim a coveted position in a temp agency, whence he returned to the gilded vocation of box-making. The company begged him to stay on full-time after extending his tenure as a temp far beyond the normal bounds, and he has since 'excelled' in that field for more years than he cares to recall.

Present day. Ward has sacrificed all the glitz and glamour of the packaging world, heroically denying its many pleasures to seek the humble station of a famous author. Or, at least, he would very much like to do that.

Midnight Mission

By Dorothy May Mercer

© 2021 D. Mercer

It must have been close to midnight. The White House was as quiet as the night before Christmas. I had not worn my watch as no jewelry is allowed here in the Navy mess-hall kitchen. My two staff seamen were feeling a bit crazy just messing around after an all-day tour. My immediate boss and the higher-ranking officers and CS (Culinary Specialists) were long gone, tucked in like babies, blissfully unaware of any impending disaster.

Seamen Sam Snead and Ute Udall sometimes play around like puppies. As a Petty Officer, the next in command, I don't mind, so long as it doesn't interfere with their duties. Sam will often put on the dog with family and friends. He has told his girlfriend that he is a White House chef, as if he worked in the executive dining room preparing exotic dishes for President Gerard Bigelow. Truthfully, it will take years of working up through the ranks, as well as serving at sea, before he will be eligible for such a posh assignment, if ever. The president chooses his own people from among the Naval Culinary Specialists who are officers in the cooking corps.

As the officer on duty, I was supervising the cleanup duties after the higher-ranking cooks left without bothering to rinse a dish or a pan. Since I was the tallest of us three, I made a point to reach high into the tall cupboard to store the largest pans. My back was turned, arms stretched overhead like a bandit, teetering on the top step of a rickety, old, wooden stepladder when Udall took advantage of my vulnerable position to snap my butt with the end of a long, wet dishtowel.

"Ack, dammit," I yelled as the pots went flying, the stepladder went one way, and I went the other, bumping in a painful heap against the dishwasher.

Udall and Snead laughed hysterically, snapping matching dishtowels, and dancing around like teenage break-dancers. Meanwhile I managed to pick myself up and check all my body parts for damage.

I was just brushing off my pants when a tall man appeared in the doorway. "Have you got any ice cream in this kitchen," he inquired.

Oh my God; it's the president! I sent up a silent prayer.

You never saw three sailors snap to attention so fast in your life! Instantly erect like saluting tin soldiers, eyes front, shoulders back, and faces straight.

"Yes, sir! Ice cream, sir!"

"Very well," said President Gerard Bigelow. "Would you mind fixing me a dish?" President Bigelow is known for his penchant for ice cream.

"Yes, sir. Right away, sir," Ute and Sam bumped into each other as they raced to the freezer. Udall opened the door. "We have chocolate, strawberry, Rocky Road, and plain vanilla, sir!"

"Just plain vanilla is fine," Bigelow replied, "But a little taste of the others will be interesting, I suppose. No harm in trying something different," he chuckled.

"Coming right up, sir."

I watched the scene in some amusement as I surreptitiously brushed off my working uniform and pasted a respectful look on my face.

 The two seamen fought each other to create a massive dish filled with artful towers of multi-colored and white confection. Together they carried their creation and placed it in front of the president as carefully as an aircraft carrier landing crew.

They stood back awaiting the president's remarks. There was a pregnant pause while a small frown wrinkled Bigelow's brow.

I broke the silence. "Is there anything more we can do for you, Mr. President, sir?" I queried.

"Um," he answered, "could I trouble you for a spoon?"

I suppressed a grin while Udall and Snead turned as red as the prize-winning scarlet flowers in the White House rose garden.

"Oh, and also," the president continued, "May I please have sprinkles with that?"

Dear God, help, I thought as I hurried to fetch the spoon and sprinkles. "Here you go, sir." I started to pour.

President Bigelow grabbed the package out of my hand. "Sorry," he said grinning like a smart-ass. "I prefer to do it myself."

"No problem, sir." I let go of the bag and backed off to watch the president carefully decorate his ice cream dish as if it was a wedding cake.

Meanwhile, Udall and Snead were doing their best to fade into the wall. Bigelow set down the sprinkles and picked up his spoon.

Good heavens, is he going to eat that here? I eyed my two compatriots and shrugged. Aloud I inquired, "Is there any other way we can help you, Mr. President?"

"That will be all, sailor," he said as—to my relief—he picked up the ice cream and turned to go.

We three waited afraid to breathe for a full thirty seconds after the swinging door had closed.

In the silence I heard the unmistakable sound of running water. "Jesus C. Christopher!" Sam Snead cried as he looked in horror at his feet.

"Dammit all, you left the water running, you idiot!" exclaimed Ute Udall.

"All hands on deck," I pronounced, as I grabbed for a mob and bucket.

Sam moaned, "What else?"

"Never mind, just get to work," I commanded in my best rendition of an officer.

Mopping and wringing ensued for what seemed like an hour but was probably less. We finished by hauling three fans out of the back room and setting them going.

I looked around. "Well, Seamen," I sighed. "I think that does it." I stretched up taller and rubbed my aching back. "What say we call it a night?"

Sam nodded tiredly, "Agreed."

Udall turned to go, "See you soon, men. Let's go. Four A.M. comes awfully early."

Barely able to wiggle, we moved through the swinging door and out into the dark, deserted dining hall.

Just then, blazing light hit our faces. I could barely discern bodies like jumping jacks, popping up from behind tables and chairs. *"What tha'?"*

What was this—the feared invasion or a civilian insurrection? Out of the corner of my eye, I noticed the melting ice cream tower.

"Surprise, surprise," they yelled, slapping each other, pointing at us, and laughing like kookaburras.

It took a few moments for my eyes and ears to adjust. And there in the midst of the raucous crowd stood the smiling first lady next to President Bigelow.

"Atten-SHUN!" commanded Lieutenant Crabtree, the Master Chef. Twenty sailors snapped to attention. Crabtree continued, "Please step forward Seamen Udall and Snead and Petty Officer Hitch."

Naturally, we obeyed like marionettes.

The first lady and the president stepped in front of us.

Bigelow shook hands with Sam and Ute. "Good job," he said.

Turning to me he said, "Congratulations, _Ensign_ Hitch. You passed the test. Please report for duty in the executive kitchen tomorrow at eight bells." He shook my hand and then added with a twinkle, "Maybe I'll see you later for a smaller helping of vanilla ice cream with sprinkles."

I gulped. "Thank you, sir," I managed with some difficulty.

The room burst into applause.

The Bigelows turned away as they started greeting people.

Udall and Snead slapped me on the back and grabbed my hand.

"Thanks," I said, "But you gobs were in on this all along, weren't you? That ice cream creation was impressive."

Sporting innocence, they gestured like three-year-olds caught in the chocolate cookie jar.

"Who me?" protested Sam.

Ute agreed. "No way, José," he claimed. "It must have been the sprinkles."

The End

NOTE:

In the Navy, the sailors who feed the rest of the troops aren't just cooks, they're Culinary Specialists (CS). They not only prepare food for their fellow sailors but for admirals, senior government executives and run the White House mess hall for the President. These sailors receive extensive training in cooking, baking, dining, and living area management. They prepare menus, order food items, operate kitchen and dining facilities, and keep records for food supplies and financial budgets. They serve as personal food service specialists for high-ranking officers both aboard ship and at shore bases.

From Little Seeds ... Hope Springs

"Grama Joins the "#WP" Generation"

By Dorothy May Mercer

© 2020 D. Mercer

(June 6, eMail to adult grandkids.)

Hi Kids!

It was mid-winter here in Michigan (April). On a trip to the store, a package of Marigold seeds called "Buy me!" (not too expensive).

Meanwhile, one day a small donation was sent to Arbor Day Foundation.

When presented with the Marigold seeds, your grandfather stifled a yawn.

Thinking on Women Power and I Am Woman, W-O-M-A N, as in "Who needs a man?" your grandmother did a fist-pump and purposed to do this herself.

Well, one thing led to another. (So far, one small Arbor Day donation and a package of Marigold seeds has cost about $200 plus a dozen trips to Ace Hardware and uncounted sore muscles.)

Next, a trip to Ace was made to procure some Miracle Grow potting soil.

Nothing but the best for Burpee seeds.

Trip #3 required a journey to Ace Hardware for some little pots for the soil, in which to plant the seeds. Despite double planting (two seeds per pot) the pots were too few.

Trips #4 and #5 to Ace were for more pots and still more pots.

- Daily watering and breathing on pots.
- Time passed; seeds came up. Oh, happy day!
- Soon there were dozens of cheery little marigold plants overflowing into more pots.

Meanwhile, an unexpected "thank-you" gift of tiny summer-flowering bulbs arrived in the mail from Arbor Day Foundation.

Trip #6 was to Ace for three treated boards, 1"X6"X8', and a package of nails. One eight-foot board was cut into two by the Helpful Hardware Man.

- Loaded boards and nails into pickup truck.
- Drove toward home.
- Turned corner.
- Stopped to retrieve boards that spewed out of the back of the vehicle.
- Stranger stopped to help. He demonstrated how to correctly load boards.
- No need to mention this to one's husband.

Trip #7 was to Ace to retrieve a blank check that had escaped out of Grandmother's purse. (Nice of them to call.)

- Laid down some black plastic.
- Nailed boards together.
- Stood back and admired the 4'X8' potential raised flower garden.
- Needed a strong man to help move heavy boards to final location.

Did Grandpas's benevolent smirk reflect approval or was it amusement?

Trip #8 to Ace Hardware, seeking advice, resulted in ten forty-pound bags of potting soil. Strong young woman loaded the bags.

- Backed up truck as close as possible to 4' X 8' raised garden.
- Poured soil into small bucket to spread inside boards, now only half full.

Trip #9 was required for ten more bags of potting soil.

- Added those, one bucket-full at a time.
- Stood back to admire garden.
- Long soak in hot tub.

Trip #10 to Ace, after careful consideration of options, the choice was smelly cow-dung fertilizer for improving the soil.

- Planted the "free gift" summer flowering bulbs in the center and a row of marigolds all around the four sides.
- Stood back and admired garden.
- Took a long hot shower.
- Fearing deer and rabbits, covered garden with used fencing and bent chicken wire.
- Next morning, inspected garden.
- Six marigolds were missing.
- A mysterious hole in garden looked large enough for a snake or mouse.
- Replaced marigolds from bulk supply.

Trip #11 to Ace was for a 25-foot roll of 48-inch chicken-wire fencing and some bamboo stakes.

Trip #12 to Ace was to exchange 25-foot roll for a 50-foot roll and more bamboo stakes, plus a board which was used in fashioning a gate.

- Stood back and admired finished flower garden.

Will soon need many vases in which to put flowers.

- Grandpa inquired, "Do you have a little space in your garden to add a few tomato plants?"

Next day: joined husband on trip to Meijer' garden center to purchase tomato plants.

- Assisted husband by digging hole and setting his two plants.

Grandpa's genuine smile said, "Come August, those will taste mighty good. I'm so proud of you."

Love,

Grams

- PUSHED SEND

Ode To A Watermelon

By Gail Sheneman

Oh, Watermelon! How I love your sweet flesh!

My favorite of all fruits, I love you best!

You melt in my mouth; your juices run out!

You fill up my tummy; Of that, there's no doubt.

I lust for more of you, but my tummy is full,

I've loved you for life; you are my jewel.

Oh, Watermelon, I am your fool!

I think I will burst, but you are so cool!

Red or yellow, either is fine,

I'll eat all of you, down to the rind

I smell you, I taste you, for you, I still pine.

Oh, Watermelon, you are All Mine!

The Tragic Day Poor Petey

Faced Execution in the Porcelain Throne

By GeAnn Powers

© 2021 G. Powers

No one remembers the events leading up to that fateful moment, least of all Petey. And no one knows why the toilet was the instrument of choice. But everyone knew why Petey was the victim: he was unquestionably the favorite. It probably wasn't even Petey's fault. Nevertheless, he paid the ultimate price for the infraction.

He may have seen his impending doom, and he may even have tried to run, but he was so small and could only move a few feet a minute. He was helpless.

Poor Petey.

The event happened over a dozen years ago now, but it unfolded just this way:

The little fellow, Petey, had only been part of our family for about a month.

Ryan had seen him in the store before Christmas and pointed him out.

"That's the one I want!" the seven-year-old proclaimed. We were engaged in our sons' favorite pastime: visiting the local toy store to look at trains. Our boys loved trains, especially a particular toy train, its friends, and the train sets marketed by a popular kids' show that dominated our sons' play and TV viewing time. The adventure-packed lives of the talking trains mesmerized our three boys.

Ryan's favorite color was green, so naturally, the green Petey engine was his favorite of all. He already had the original Petey engine; the Petey covered with icicles from the snow episode, and a painted chocolate covered Petey from the chocolate show. Now, here before him was the most awesome engine of all: a battery powered Petey that could pull freight cars all by itself! A working light shone out above this engine's smiling face.

We were generous parents, so we were happy to give Ryan a fantastic battery powered Petey for Christmas. The little train ruled the playroom as he chugged along the wooden tracks that dominated the space, pulling a long line of cars behind him and lighting the way for all to see.

That lasted about a month.

Maybe it was the persistent proud grin on Petey's face or the fact that he was the only battery-powered engine in a train yard full of powerless wooden companions. Perhaps it was Ryan telling his little brother one more time, "No, I don't want to play with you right now." Whatever the reason, three-year-old Jo snatched up the helpless little engine and ran into the bathroom. Jo slammed the door in a screaming Ryan's face and flushed the toilet.

Poor Petey.

We all ran to see why Ryan was crying and gazed into the porcelain bowl, beseeching it to show us what happened. But the evidence was gone–washed down the drain.

Poor, poor Petey.

Ryan was inconsolable. His favorite toy had met its demise at the hands of his "evil" younger brother. Ten-year-old Chris offered up his prize circus train set. But Ryan did not stop wailing. I admonished the culprit. Nevertheless, all the crying, scolding, and token circus trains in the world could not bring Petey back.

And worst yet, the toilet was now clogged.

Terry, the local handyman, had rewired our kitchen, installed our air-conditioning, and unstopped more drains than a family with three boys could produce. If anyone could get the toilet working again, it was superhuman Terry.

Terry came with his tools: a plunger, Drano, and a coat hanger, but the toilet remained clogged. Terry sighed in resignation, hung a "Do Not Use" sign across the porcelain commode, and promised to return the next day.

We sent thank you prayers up to heaven because we had a second bathroom.

Late that night, my husband called me into the unusable bathroom.

"You didn't use it, did you?" I questioned.

"No but look!"

He flipped off the lights.

From deep inside the recesses of the toilet's dark cave, there came a faint glow. Trapped in a watery grave, Petey was signaling to us. "Here I am! Help! Please get me out!" the light seemed to say. Somewhere from the dark abyss, Petey's light shown on, and the tiny wheels kept turning, trying to get back to us.

Helplessly, my husband and I shrugged and stared at each other. There was no way to reach the little train.

Poor, poor Petey. He was a trooper to the end.

As promised, the next day, Terry returned. He dismantled the toilet, pulled it up off the floor, and flipped it over. Reaching deep into the gooseneck water channel, Terry searched around for a few seconds. He pulled out a dripping but triumphant Petey, whom he wrapped in a paper towel like a burial shroud.

"Here you go!" he said, with a big grin, and handed the damp bundle to me.

I peeled back the paper covering and examined Petey. He was scratched up but otherwise seemed fine. I pushed the button on the engine cabin. Nothing happened. His light had gone out, his little wheels motionless. Ryan wailed in grief.

Poor, dear Petey.

Despite his tragic fate, I removed Petey's battery, scrubbed him up with an old toothbrush, and set him on the windowsill to dry. A few days later, I popped in a fresh battery and tried the button again. Petey's light sprang to life, and his wheels whizzed around in circles, racing along an imaginary track. He smiled up at me with his frozen grin. Why had I ever doubted him?

"Ryan!" I called. The seven-year-old came running. He stopped in his tracks when he saw his beloved train and heard the whirling of its minuscule battery motor cranking the tiny axles. Ryan's smile grew even wider than Petey's.

I watched little Petey that day cheerfully chugging along the tracks, going through tunnels, over bridges, and under chairs. He grinned the whole time and didn't even mind when Jo asked for a turn to play with him. Ryan and his little brother were friends again, and Petey was glad to be back where he belonged.

Dear Petey, you silly little hunk of metal and plastic. There you go persevering with a smile through the greatest of hardships, shining a light when there is no hope in sight, staging a comeback when everyone else has given up in despair, and forgiving the one who caused it all.

Oh, Petey! You are my hero.

About the Author—GeAnn Powers

GeAnn is married, and lives in Kentwood, Michigan. Her adorable dog, Rory, is a mixed breed she fondly calls a "chi-watty."

Her charming children's story about Petey, the toy train, it indicative of GeAnn Power's prolific writing ability. Several of her books have been featured on Amazon.com, among them her Firefly collection and *I Love You Like Salt.*

Click or go here for links to her Amazon page:

Amazon.com : GeAnn Powers

Remember the Year – 2020

By Dorothy May Mercer

January was icy

And freezing, Oh no!

February was traveling

Downhill over snow.

In March we were packing

For beaches and fishing

Back home in April

For showers, we're wishing.

In May we dismay

As our new plants get frosted.

In June we delight

In marshmallows toasted.

July brings a blowfly

Dispatched with a swatter.

In August we skim

Over waves and warm water.

September, remember

To write to your mother.

October is busy

One way or another.

November–get ready

To vote, plus Thanksgiving.

December is wrapping

And writing and posting

Letters and packages

Numerous mailings.

Already it's New Year's.

Remember the cruel tears

The smiles and the kisses,

Hugs, and good wishes?

Here's to your wealth,

Good times, and good health.

Where do the years go?

Can't say that I know.

My Daughter's Memory

By Chuck Houghton

It's quiet now on the deck.
Her sharp laugh is now checked.
The reasons for it still abound.
It's quiet now. The sound has drowned.

I will always hear her jingle.
It's quiet now, but I still feel a tingle.
It's easy to smile at my memories.
It's quiet now. She's hiding in the trees.

Because of her, my life was never empty.
It's quiet now, but she is still here with me.
I walk the two-track alone.
It's quiet now, but nature will atone.

Please notice, my one hand reaches out.
It's quiet now. Our big shadow has clout.
Yes, we've parted, but we're still together.
It's quiet now, but that makes it better.

What I feel makes me glad.

It's quiet now, and I'm still her dad.

My Lady Catalpa

By Gail Sheneman

Her blossoms are like orchids

So pure and so white,

Lady Catalpa shines in the night.

After her blossoms are gone,

Lady Catalpa's work is not done.

Out sprout the beans so long and so green

Falling to the ground

Turning all brown

And making much work for the mowing machine.

Yes, Lady Catalpa is grand

Making an elegant stand.

Catalpa, Catalpa, Queen of the trees

The most beautiful tree in the land.

She towers over all the other trees.

Treating the eyes of anyone who sees.

Showing her leaves of a chartreuse green

Lady Catalpa is still the queen!

About the Author—Gail Sheneman

Many-talented author, Gail Weissert-Sheneman, lives in Stanton, Michigan with her husband, Carl, and their two pet cats, pastel calico Princess Heidi, and Maine Coon Buddy. She keeps busy with church work, relatives, Red Hat Lady Bugs, GFWC Edmore Women's Club and numerous friends and charities. Her hobbies are painting, making gift baskets, flower arrangements, singing, dancing, writing and her many collections, which give her home the appearance of a museum.

Gail hopes to publish at least two books in the coming year.

Recently she published a charming and informative childrens' book, available on Amazon.com, The Princess and the Little Elephant (Click Here).

The fully, beautifully illustrated, printed storybook is available on Amazon.com. $11.99; please click the cover or go here: The Princess and the Little Elephant: Sheneman, Gail: 9781623290689: Amazon.com: Books

Temptation

By Netty Ejike

Excerpt from *Driven Wild* by Netty Ejike, a steamy romance, coming soon.

© 2021 N. Ejike

Thorne Lorenzo's sensitive ears picked up the hearty girlish ring of *her* laughter from the next room, and his breath caught in his throat, his body quickening in response to the mere sound, his heart beginning to pump unevenly.

It was that bad!

Thorne bit back a savage curse and raked an unsteady hand through his thick, jet-black hair, slightly longer than usual because he had not had time for a cut.

There was no need to know if *she* was the one. Her voice was imprinted on his brain.

His chocolate brown eyes narrowed to slits as her gorgeous face appeared in his mind's eye, followed by the shape of her hands—those slim hands of which he had often dreamed.

Thorne bit hard on his thin lower lip when he felt the seams of his pants stretch.

"Louse," he muttered under his breath, tasting blood from his lip.

He stabbed a finger on the intercom resting on the left corner of his walnut desk.

His PA's bubbly voice came on the line, "Sir?"

"Shut the connecting door," Thorne barked. "This is the last time I'll warn you about it."

"I'm sorry, sir," came the repentant voice.

A second later, Thorne heard the soft click of the door. He glared at the closed door, but that did not lessen his fury.

And yes, he was furious with himself for allowing a slip of a girl to affect him like no other woman.

And he had known many.

Thorne Lorenzo cursed again and turned to his laptop, but instead of the tables and graphs on the screen, his eyes could only see a slim, shapely body with a face made for the angels.

About the Author—Netty Ejike

Prolific author, Netty Ejike, started writing at the age of twelve, after reading her first Mills and Boon; thus living up to her nickname, Romantia. Born in Enugu, Nigeria, she studied Psychology at the University of Nigeria and received Elizabeth Lord's award for being the best female graduate from the department. This knowledge, gained in her studies, is reflected in her writing, where the reader will meet some deep and fascinating characters.

Netty's working experience cut across several career roles as an agent in a travel agency, an admin. officer in a corporate company, and a marketing manager in a hotel. Through this experience she met even more "characters."

At last, her heart's desire has come true. She is now a full-time writer, with her own imprint: DeRafelo Romance. Netty has written more than two dozen novels, each with its own setting, characters, and religious inclinations. Having no fear of tackling difficult subjects such as sexual assault and dysfunction, cultural curses, and beliefs, she sets her exotic romances in interesting and intriguing world settings.

Netty Ejike has served as the Chairperson of the Association of Nigerian Authors, Enugu State Chapter. And now lives in Enugu with her beloved husband and publisher, Chijioke, their two sons and two daughters.

For more information go to Amazon.com : Netty Ejike

Two Poems

By Linda Hawley

©2021 L. Hawley

The Memory List

Years gone by

Make me sigh

Refuse to die

Pie in the sky

Lost friends

Road has bends

Send tens of pens

Memories dear

Without a tear

Hold you near

With little fear

Better times

With more than dimes

Lemons and limes

Sit here and pine

Remember when

You were ten

The chick and hen

Were in their pen

        We were young

        Songs were sung

        Friends among

        We hung; had fun

                Happier days

                It's all a haze

                Walk thru the maze

                This was a phase

Walnuts

Out here with one
thousand walnuts
Small ones, black
ones, yellow and green
And there are still
more up there

They keep falling.

Mature ones are two inches wide
One could hit me on the head
It may knock me out
Someone will find me Sunday morning.

What will this do to my allergies?
Takes ninety minutes to rake
Gather up in a bucket and
Dump in the wheelbarrow.

Travel to the backyard and
Deposit under bushes
Where they will be out of sight
Squirrels may still find them.

Next year the tree will produce no walnuts
I can rest up 'til twenty-twenty-three.

About the Author—Linda Hawley

Linda Hawley was inspired to write after reading two poetry books her mother, Norma Hawley, had published. She remembers stories from her childhood while growing up in Lakeview, Michigan. Writing down these stories from the 1950s and 1960s has been rewarding.

During her attendance with the Tamarack Writers' Group, she learned more about poetry and began writing poems. She now has many poems to her credit.

Like other members of the group, Linda spends much of her time in service to others without realizing it is special or thinking of herself. Linda's church and her friends often receive beautiful, original gifts created from her hobbies of crocheting and embroidering.

Along with taking walks in Lakeview, Linda enjoys playing the piano.

The Bear

By Gerald W. Kinsey

Excerpt from *"Him and Her,"* A Story About Survival in the Artic, by Gerald W. Kinsey, available on Amazon.

© 2020 G. Kinsey

Over the next few days they tried to catch fish. The new spear helped some, but they were only able to get enough to keep from starving. The sea was beginning to form ice crystals. It would only be a few more days before it froze over. Then it would be even harder to obtain enough to survive, and the days were getting shorter. In another month or two the sun would not rise at all. The temperatures were frequently dropping below zero at night, and they were still not even near the coldest part of the winter. Even with the progress they had made, the only real question was whether they would die from freezing or starving.

The only time of day they could stand to be outside was during the early afternoon. Even then a couple hours were all they could bear. The shelter was not much warmer, but it was the best they had. During the brief time they were out in the cold, they tried to focus all their attention on fishing. That is why they didn't notice the danger until it was too late.

He was concentrating on getting the net under a medium sized cod when he heard her scream. He looked up and saw that his worst fears had been realized. A polar bear had swum ashore on the other side of the island and was approaching them. It was between them and their igloo. There was no escape. Instinctively he grabbed the spear and stepped between her and the bear. Maybe if he could distract it, she could get around the bear and make it to the shelter. That would only delay her death a short time, but he had to do what he could.

The Polar Bear drawing by Olivia Kinsey

He told her to try to circle around while he waved the spear in the bear's face. She got part way when the bear attacked him. He ran back a few steps and then turned to face it. It was not full grown. When it stood on its hind legs, it was about six feet tall. That is to say it was a six foot, two hundred pound killing machine that was hungry after its long swim. Would he have any chance against it with his puny spear? He didn't know, but he had no choice but to try.

He tried to keep the spear between him and the bear. If there was a chance, maybe he could get in a lucky jab. Luck was not with him. Almost faster than he could see, the bear hit him on the chest with its forepaw. He dropped to the ground motionless.

She looked on, too terrified to move. He had warned her of the danger of polar bears, and now she had seen the bear kill him with just one quick blow. She knew she would be next. What difference did it make? She knew she could not survive without him. After all their efforts to stay alive, their lives had ended abruptly with the arrival of this bear.

Suddenly, she didn't care anymore about trying to avoid death. She knew she couldn't anyway. All she could think of was that this bear had taken away what little chance of life she had. Now she was angry. There was no point in trying to escape. She knew she couldn't do anything to harm the bear, but she would at least take out her frustrations on it before she died.

The bear was standing over the man to make sure he was dead. She ran at it in a fit of rage. The bear certainly had not expected an attack from anything so small and weak. Polar bears have no enemies. They are the masters of their entire world. No one can challenge them, and yet this little creature was pounding on its back. It didn't hurt at all. The bear was more surprised than anything else. It turned around to see what was happening. She continued to beat on it. The bear finally realized it was being attacked. What presumption! No one attacks a polar bear. It rose again on its hind legs and prepared to kill this foolish attacker. It would only take one swipe of its paw.

The man was not dead. He was only stunned by the blow he had received. His chest hurt, but no ribs had been broken. He looked up to see the bear standing over her. In a moment she would be killed. He had no thought of being a hero. He was a man, and a woman was in imminent danger of death. There was only one thing to do. He grabbed his spear and rushed toward the bear. Its back was toward him. With all his strength he stabbed the spear into the bear's back.

Either by luck or by providence, the spearhead landed right in the bear's spine. It instantly dropped to the ground. He yanked out the spear and stepped back. The bear howled in pain and rage. It tried to rise to destroy the creature that had caused him the pain, but its hind legs would not respond. It tried again. It couldn't stand up. It still would not let the offense go unpunished.

Using its front legs, the bear pawed its way toward the man. He jumped back. Even a badly wounded bear can cause instant death. The bear tried again to rise, but to no effect. It lunged toward the man again. Even in its partly paralyzed condition, the bear almost caught him. This happened a couple more times. He tried to think what to do. The bear was disabled, but it was far from dead. Should he just try to stay away from the beast or try to kill it? It would not die for a long time if at all. If he tried to kill it, he might be killed.

He tried to stay out of range for a while. Then he had an idea. He had been able to stab the bear before because she had distracted it. Maybe they could use the same tactic again. He called to her to throw a rock at it. When she did, the bear turned around to see what was happening. He stepped toward it cautiously. Then the bear turned back to see him within range of its powerful front legs. This was its chance to kill the thing that had caused it so much trouble.

It gave a wrathful growl before making the kill. The man saw his chance and thrust his spear into the bear's mouth. The tip punctured the main artery going to the head. Blood poured out of its mouth. He jumped back, leaving the spear where it had landed. The bear pawed at the spear in an attempt to dislodge it. It was to no avail. The wound would prove fatal in a few minutes, as the bear's lifeblood gushed out. There was nothing to do now but wait for the loss of blood to have its effect. He stepped back to watch at a safe distance. He knew that even a badly wounded bear was still very dangerous.

He suddenly realized that he was shaking. Was it the cold, or was it the extreme danger they had just faced? Then he remembered her. Was she all right? She was standing there in a daze. She didn't seem to have been harmed physically, but it went without saying that she was greatly shaken by the experience.

"Are you okay?" he asked.

She didn't answer at first. Then she said weakly, "Yes."

He wasn't sure if she even heard him. He returned his attention to the bear. It was becoming weaker by the minute. Taking a chance, he approached. It might spring back to life at any time. Grabbing the spear, he gave it a quick pull. If the bear had had hands, it might have been able to dislodge the spear. That probably would have only accelerated the loss of blood. Anyway, he was able to retrieve his spear. He stood there for a few more minutes with the spear in hand just in case. When the bear seemed to be still, he came closer and prodded it to see if there was any life yet. When he was satisfied that it was really dead, he relaxed.

He was still shaking. They had nearly been killed. She slowly approached. When she looked at the bear, she saw all the blood. It disgusted her.

"You killed the poor animal. That's awful."

He couldn't believe his ears. That "poor animal" had nearly killed both of them, and now all she cared about was the fact that he had killed it. Maybe she would have preferred to be killed herself. All the time they had been there she had done nothing but complain. She would have been dead a long time already if it were not for him, and now she was condemning him for killing a bear that almost killed them. How could she be so stupid? How about a little appreciation for saving her life! He had tried to be patient with her, and this was the response he got. He was fed up with it, and he didn't want to take any more.

"Look, you dumb blond, don't you understand what this means?"

"Don't call me that."

"Okay, I'm sorry. It just slipped out."

"Well, if it slipped out, you must have been thinking it."

"Hey, I said I'm sorry."

"You men are all alike. You think just because a girl has blond hair she can't have any brains. What about men with blond hair? Do they have brains? You think you are so superior. I'm just as smart as you. You are nothing but an egotistical, male chauvinist pig, and I hate..." She stopped in the middle of her tirade. "Wait a minute. What did you just say?"

"I said I'm sorry I called you a dumb blond."

"No, I mean the other."

"What?"

"You said, 'don't you understand what this means?' What are you talking about?"

How could she be so dense? He was tempted to ask, but he didn't want another tongue-lashing.

Apparently he would have to spell it out for her. Trying to control himself, he said, "Look at the bear."

"I don't want to."

"Come on. Look."

Reluctantly, she complied.

"What do you see?"

"A pitiful animal you killed and a lot of blood. I hate blood."

Maybe he should have let the bear kill her. But no. That would not be right, and he really didn't want her dead. Biting his tongue, he said, "What you ought to be seeing is a hundred pounds of meat, a warm fur coat and bones to use for tools, weapons and a sled."

Slowly it began to sink in. The bear would enable them to survive the winter. Still in a bit of a daze, she said softly to herself, "I really am a dumb blond." When she realized what she had just said, she tried to back-paddle. "What I mean is...that is...well, yes. I see what you mean. A hundred pounds of meat. Yes, that would make about four hundred quarter-pounders. There are two of us. That means two hundred each. Yes, that should be enough to get us through the winter. The fur coat will keep us from freezing. The bones should help. Yes, I see. You are quite right. My thought exactly." She realized she was only making herself look more foolish. She concluded, "Okay, I'll shut up now."

He looked at her, and she looked at him. Then he began to smile. She smiled too. Then he laughed. Then she laughed. They both realized their argument was really just a result of the extreme stress they had been under.

He said, "I'll try to remember not to call you a dumb blond again."

"And I really don't think you are a male chauvinist pig, just a male chauvinist." They both laughed again.

So it was that the bear who could have been the cause of their death became the means of their life.

About the Author—Gerald Kinsey

Gerald "Jake" Kinsey has been a dairy farmer, mobile home park operator, husband, father, grandfather and newspaper carrier. Currently, he is a newspaper publisher of the Lakeview Area News, for which he writes an editorial each week. Those articles are laced with his wry sense of humor.

Recently he also became an author. His first book, _The Poor, Rich Man_ is a story based on the Biblical account of the rich, young ruler.

The author has long been interested in the Arctic and the hardy people who have survived there for centuries. _Him and Her_ is a fictional story about two people who are abandoned on an Arctic Island by an evil crime boss. The reader will learn many interesting facts about the Arctic while enjoying the interaction of these two fascinating people.

133

Jake is one of the founding members of Tamarack Writers' Group. In keeping with their tradition, he spends time in various causes and service to others. He has a strong interest in prison ministries, particularly for the innocent and mistakenly imprisoned. He is busy writing his third book, a true-crime story about a man who has been wrongly accused and incarcerated for life.

For a link to Gerald's books, go here Amazon.com : Gerald Kinsey.

The Crown

By Wendye Savage

Excerpt from : *What's in Your Purse*" : A Guide for Women's Wellness

Glowing from within itself

This radiant beam of light

Created and designed by

The personal triumphs of life.

Created in the fire

Tested in its flames

From within a woman's heart

Purpose pushes from her pain.

You wonder how she gets back up

After being knocked down to the ground.

Well, God is walking with her

And His power is in her crown.

If her tiara slips and falls

Grace shall be found

For God is walking with her

And His power is in her crown.

About the Author- Wendye Savage

Wendye Savage is an author, poet, mental health advocate, certified life coach, inspirational speaker, overcomer, and Woman of God.

Wendye has been delivered from a history of major depression, mental and sexual abuse, low self-esteem and confidence, hatred and unforgiveness.

Her calling is to aid other women challenged with the obstacles she has overcome.

Wendye has shared her testimony through radio, television, magazine, and her latest book, a self-help guide, entitled, What's in Your Purse?

Wendye plans to open her life coach practice, Igniting Her Worth LLC, in the fall of 2021. Her practice is geared toward aiding women who struggle with self-esteem and low self-confidence.

wendye_savage@yahoo.com

https://www.amazon.com/Whats-Your-Purse-Womens-Wellness/dp/1728361982/ref=tmm_pap_swatch_0?_encoding=UTF8&qid=1605835268&sr=1-1

The First Fawn of the Year

By Dorothy May Mercer

© 2020 D. Merceer

Oh, look, honey. There's a fawn," I cried. It was the first fawn of the year.

The fiddlehead ferns had been out for a week, the traditional harbinger of births for our wild deer population. The mother deer keeps the infant hidden for several days until finally, the rambunctious babies start to venture out. It was time.

It is always exciting to see the cute little animals with their big eyes, sensitive ears, and light spots on caramel-colored fur. But the first fawn of the year is an event that will stop traffic or send the family members running to a window. It is even better than spotting the first robin or crocus. We know that Summer is near; life has returned after a long dreary winter.

On this day, we were in our car, driving East on M-20. My husband was in the driver's seat beside me. We had been chatting and enjoying the beautiful countryside and bluebird weather. Unfortunately, traffic was heavier than usual. A large black pickup truck followed close behind. Just then, we spotted the lone fawn standing beside the road, with no mother in sight.

My husband started to slow the car, mindful of both the fawn and the truck on our rear bumper. In a split second, I could see the fawn's face, and I knew somehow what he was thinking. Time stood still. In horror, I yelled, "No-no, baby," as if I thought he could hear and obey me.

In an instant, the terrified animal dashed directly in front of us. '

"OH NO!!!" I screamed. And then, I heard the sickening thump as our bumper connected with his little body.

My husband, bless him, maintained control as I burst into tears. It was over so fast. All he could do was drive on in stunned silence.

Animals die on the road every hour of every day in Michigan. More than once, we have hit an adult deer with the resulting significant damage to our vehicle. It is a family joke to report, "Well, call the insurance company; I did it again—I went deer hunting with a two-ton automobile."

But this deer/auto collision left no marks in the paint; it only dented our hearts.

The Cat and the Ant

By Dorothy May Mercer

"Kitty" understands my commands. However, to him they are merely suggestions, which he can consider. One can almost see the idea going around in his brain. For instance I may say, "Come here, Kitty" and pat my lap. In this case he may look, banefully, at my lap and quietly turn away. After pacing the room, tail in the air, he may return and jump gracefully onto my lap, offering his royal self for a head-scratch before leaving. Thus, he has let me know it was not just his decision, it was his idea in the first place.

There is one exception to this behavior—our "never-fail" bedtime routine. He knows when it is ten o'clock. As soon as he sees Dave and I close and lock the doors and turn off the TV and lights, he stations himself in the middle of the kitchen floor, waiting patiently for me to call him, "C'm 'ere, Kitty," I call, as I rattle his package of cat treats. "It's treat-time," I trill. Rarely do I need to call him twice, as he knows he will get two of his favorite treats, tossed onto the floor of his room where I shut him in for the night. God bless the makers of cat treats.

After months with no bedtime problems, imagine my consternation Tuesday night at 10:15 when I repeatedly called him, "Treat-time, Kitty, where are you? C'mon Kitty," I called, ever more loudly.

No answer.

I switched the light back on and walked the three paces into the kitchen. There he was, ignoring my pleas, totally absorbed with a wonderful new toy, batting it back and forth with his paw. It was his first experience with a black ant. The more it scurried away, the more fascinated he became.

We would still be there, at loggerheads, if the ant had not made a break for it and headed directly into Kitty's room with Kitty right behind.

Quickly I closed the door, lest the two of them escape. On second thought, I opened the door barely long enough to toss in two cat treats. "Here's your treat," I said, closing the door. "G'night, Kitty."

I wonder if he noticed.

The Premonition

By Dorothy May Mercer

Rahani's eyes darted nervously out the window at the tarmac. The sound of the airplane's engines roared in her ears. Her hands gripped the armrests as if they could somehow save her if the worst should happen. A wispy scent of jet fuel caused her seatmate to sneeze. "Pardon me," he said. Rahani nodded.

Rahani knew the routine. She had lived through it plenty of times. Why should she feel uneasy about this flight? Was it the disturbing dream—the one that kept coming back? *Of course not, silly woman*, she thought, half-smiling at her seatmate.

The plane shuddered like a caged lion as the brakes restrained it from leaping forth. White-hot vapor shot from the engines.

Rahani felt the air stir as the flight attendant swept by, making one last inspection before buckling herself into the jump-seat, prepared for takeoff. Unconsciously Rahani wiggled her butt back in the seat, tightened the seatbelt securely across her lap, and poked one toe into the large bag tucked under the seat in front of her.

Mentally, she ticked off her checklist, one more time. Her carryon bag was crammed into the overhead bin, and her two large suitcases were safely stowed in the yawning belly of the aircraft. One of those bags contained her shoes, two-weeks' worth of soiled laundry and several items of clothing which she had not worn. Why did she always pack more than she would need? The other smaller bag contained mementos of her visit and the presents she was taking home to her family back in Toronto. Rahani closed her eyes and pictured the looks on their dear faces as each one opened his or her gift. How she missed them!

The visit with her relatives in Tehran had been taxing, especially the time with her aging mother. Rahani knew it might be the last. But this country was no longer home. Her heart was exactly six-thousand, one-hundred fifty miles away.

Moments ago, she had obeyed the loudspeaker's recorded voice speaking in two languages before the final orders in English. "Welcome aboard this Ukrainian International Airlines flight for London, England, stopping in Kiev, Ukraine, and continuing on to Toronto Canada. Please secure your seatbelts, place all parcels under the seat in front of you, and turn off all electronic devices."

"I have to hang up now," Rahani spoke quietly into her cell phone.

"You'll be fine," assured her husband, Paul. "Try to relax, darling. I'll see you in a few hours." He knew how worried she must be about the latest fracas between Iran and the United States. Threats and missiles had been flying during the last eight hours. Her flight was one of the few commercial airlines still operating out of Iman Khomeni International Airport in Shahedshahr, southwest of the capital city of Tehran.

Although Rahani was saying nothing about her frightening dream, Paul knew her too well. Something in her tone of voice telegraphed the anxiety she felt. He continued trying to reassure her, calm her down and make her laugh a bit. "The kids and I have a surprise for you when you arrive home," he offered.

"Yeah, I'll just bet you have a surprise," she countered. "Soiled laundry piled everywhere and kitchen counters full of dirty dishes."

"Not true, not true! You wound me," he chortled. "We've been good. Everything is truly shipshape. I've collected all the laundry in one place, and the kids helped me clear the table and put everything in the sink." He laughed again. "Just kidding."

"Ha! Let's hope so," she retorted. "Gotta go. Love you," she added.

"Love you back," he replied.

"Good bye."

"Bye for now. Stay safe."

Rahani held the phone close to her heart, reluctant to let go. Slowly she clicked it onto airplane mode, tucked it away into the pocket, leaned back and sighed.

Her mind returned to reality as the Boeing 727-800 began to move. Down the runway it roared, faster and faster. Rahani's head pressed back into the seat.

Fists taut,

Eyes tight,

Body braced.

Unseen, out the window the airport passed in a blur. Powerful jet engines, designed by CFM International, seemed able to pull a million tons of cargo off the ground with ease. As soon as the pilots felt the ground fall away, they touched controls which would adjust the flaps, and suck the wheels into the guts of the plane.

They were flying.

A beautiful thing,

Like always.

Slowly, Rahani released the breath she was holding. As the cabin lights dimmed, she opened her eyes and gazed out the window at the sight of the sparkling city, rapidly receding into a spider web of tiny lights. For a moment the eerie glow flowing upward from the city disappeared into a gray canvas as the airplane entered a cloud, reminiscent of a time in Hades before bursting into glorious, heavenly starlight. She relaxed her grip and savored the moment, inhaling the peace.

Fortunately, she did not see the deadly SA-15 ground-to-air missiles as they launched and soared upward, containing enough shrapnel to shred their target into a billion bloody pieces.

Rahani never knew what hit her.

~~~~~~~~~~~~~~

Author's Note:

The story, *The Premonition,* is fiction-based-on-facts. We like to shorten the genre to "faction."

We postulated, "What could it have been like–felt like–for a woman to be on the above airplane flight?"

While certain details in this story are reminiscent of an actual airline disaster, the characters, their experience and their circumstances are fictional and are entirely created in the author's imagination.

For more of the author's writings in this genre see *Midnight Mission*, and/or go to:

www.MercerPublications.com or search her name on Amazon.com.

© Ebrahim Noroozi/AP

Rescue workers inspect the scene where a Ukrainian plane crashed in Shahedshahr, southwest of the capital Tehran, Iran, Wednesday, Jan. 8, 2020. A Ukrainian airplane with more than 170 people crashed on Wednesday shortly after takeoff from Tehran's main airport, killing all onboard, [including fifty-seven Canadians]. (AP Photo/Ebrahim Noroozi)

Courtesy of CNN.com.

The Temptress

By Joe Tilton

©2020 J. Tilton

Chapter One 1882

"That was mighty good preaching," the old, bearded man told me. He shook my hand vigorously then squinted to see the door as he shuffled off.

"One of the most blessed, brush-arbor meetings, Brother Carl. You're such a fine young man. Say, why are you not married-up with some God-fearing young Christian woman?" the old lady asked. She leaned a little closer and continued, "You know, the devil can really work on a man your age if he's not married."

Instead of waiting for a reply, she shook her head as if disgusted, then followed the old man.

The sawdust floor of pine and cedar was worn thin at the door. I looked up to see the last one in line.

"Thank you for waiting so long," I said to the young woman. "God bless you lady. I saw you sitting over there while I was preaching. Your smiles sure helped my spirits." I grinned properly then said, "Now, what's your name?"

"Beth, Beth May. Actually, I'm widowed. There's no social life up here in New York, so close to

Canada, so I attend gospel meetings Your preaching was wonderful, but I'm a member of..."

"It doesn't matter where you attend church. We're just God's children out here. Glad you came Will you be so kind as to come again tomorrow night?" I asked with anticipation.

"Well," she said very softly, "if you think I should."

"Oh, yes, I really think you should," I said quietly and preacher-like. "Revelation–yes, ma'am, I'm preaching on Revelation tomorrow, and you'll certainly enjoy it."

There was a shine in her auburn hair I hadn't noticed before. A couple of men wearing wide-brimmed black hats were blowing out fires in the coal-oil lamps. Globes and metal squeaked. It didn't matter that the room was darkening; her face glowed with a smile that had distracted me from my message all evening. Silence halted time. My gaze fixed on her beautiful teeth. Her tongue touched the corner of her mouth. I gasped for air then felt foolish for losing my composure. I had to say something to save the moment.

"I... Well. Mrs. May, I really..."

"Beth, Brother Carl. Call me Beth."

"Well, Miss Beth, I look forward to seeing you again."

The slender lady leaned closer. I caught a delicate scent of her perfume and felt dampness trickle from my arm pits. She whispered, "The pleasure will be all mine, Reverend Carl."

"Are you ready to go?" a shrill voice asked from somewhere in the darkness.

"Be right there!" I answered and pulled my black wool coat closed.

"Sounds like you're staying with the Tilley's," Beth said.

"Well, yes I am."

She leaned closer again and whispered, "Their daughter; be careful. She's a little…" She tapped her head to indicate a mental problem.

I departed leaving Beth to stand alone. The moon was full, but its silver glow was no match for the black horse and buggy. It was easy to see the ground, but my transportation appeared in silhouette.

It was the Lord, I guess, that made me turn around to look. Just like Lot's wife, I froze in my tracks for a second, taking in the image of her standing there against the soft, golden glow of the last few lamps still lit. Dust from the floor nearly settled making a smoke-like haze around Beth's feet.

Must be one of Your angles. I whispered a prayer.

"Brother Carl, are you coming?!" Sister Tilley shrilled.

I must have jumped. Their daughter laughed and giggled for a moment, and then stopped.

"We will have sassafras tea and pudding when we get to our place," I heard Sister Tilley say in her high-pitched tones. "You DO like pudding," she insisted. "You'd better."

"Here, ride shotgun, preacher," Mr. Tilley offered.

"Oh, Daddy, let him sit back here with me," the girl of fifteen or sixteen whined.

Beth's warning about the girl flashed in my mind, and so I acted as if I didn't hear the invitation to sit inside.

"We've never had anybody preach a meeting for us from Mexico, New York," he started. "Your family settled up there years ago, I hear."

"We did. It was 1622 that my clan cleared enough timber to build a place. The old house is still there after more than two-hundred-sixty years."

The driver whistled and snapped the reins. The big horse obeyed abruptly, jerking us back in our seats. We rode in silence under the moonlight for several miles as harnesses and rigging jingled with each stride. Easy breezes swept our faces. Evergreens and pines bowed to waves of wind above.

To keep from appearing rude, I spoke, "It sure is nice of you to provide a place during the meeting."

"Anything for God's men," he replied. "We've had other preachers stay with us. They seem to enjoy our place. Guess they like my wife's pudding."

The buggy rattled down to a stream and we crossed slowly. I put my hands through the space between the back of the driver's seat to hold on. Instead of finding wood when I reached down, I felt soft, smooth skin. I jerked away and turned back to look. The man's daughter was looking up at me with a soft moon-lit smile.

"Are you well?" the driver asked.

"Oh, sure; thought I'd dropped my Bible, but it's here," I lied.

We topped a small hill and continued a short distance to a gate.

"Here we are. Hold the reins while I open it."

"No, I'll get the gate, Brother Tilley."

My host drove through while I waited. The girl watched me carefully then yelled, "Wait Daddy, don't leave him behind," just before he reined the horse and buggy to a stop.

I think you'd better help me with this one, Lord, I prayed while climbing aboard.

"Make yourself at home, Reverend Carl. I'll get the pudding. It's bread pudding. I've been working on it for days," Mrs. Tilley said as we climbed the porch steps.

The log cabin had two rooms. The kitchen featured a new, modern wood stove in the corner with pots and pans hanging on the wall around it. Mr. Tilley had dug a well in the corner so they didn't have to go outside for water. There were no beds in the first room. I guessed they all slept in the other one.

"Welcome to our place, preacher; here, sit in my rocker and relax. We have an extra featherbed. I'll get it for you and put it right there," he said, pointing to a corner near a massive wooden table.

The teenage girl glanced at the spot where my bed would be, looked at her mother to see that she was busy, then stared into my eyes. I couldn't help it; I smiled.

~~~~~

About the Author—Joe Tilton

Posting in "About me," Joseph Tilton has written these few words about himself: "I'm a writer at Lakeview Area News, living in Lakeview, Michigan. I am a fan of Freedom, free enterprise, and civility. I'm also interested in peace and patience."

This doesn't begin to tell you the volumes that could be written about Joe's amazing accomplishments, burning interests, opinions, crusades, and challenges.

As a writer Joe has one published book that we know of, *Apocalypse, the Ultimate Battle for the Soul of Humanity,* and two as yet unpublished: a weighty tome, and adventurous historical novel *Reverend Carl,* and his newest passion, *Giant Leap, for Mankind,* in which Joe explores the near and distant future, and proposes repeated visits to target planets.

In recent years, Joe has been a busy reporter for the *Lakeview Area News,* covering the local Courts and more. Several of his articles have appeared in the award-winning weekly newspaper.

Joe is a founding member and beloved contributor to the Tamarack Writers' Group. Several of his stories appear in their annual anthologies.

For the past year, Joe has been sidelined, courageously battling a serious health issue. We wish him well, a long life and speedy return to good health.

Joe lives, with his wife Connie, in Lakeview, Michigan.

Princess Elizabella's Problem

By Gail Sheneman

Excerpt from *The Princess and the Little Elephant,* a children's book, available in paperback on Amazon.com.

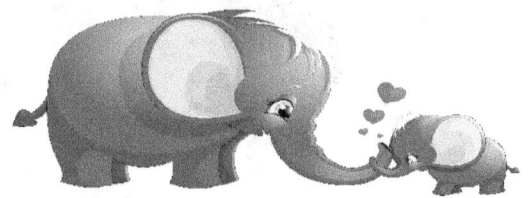

CHAPTER ONE

Once upon a time, somewhere in a land far away, there lived a princess whose name was Elizabella with a "z." She and her family lived on an island in the Atlantic Ocean called Flores, which is part of the

Azores, an archipelago of islands off Portugal. The island was incredibly beautiful, covered with grassy hills, extinct volcanoes, deep valleys, and high peaks. Among the cliffs, carved by grottoes, there were hot springs and lagoons bordered by a profusion of wildflowers, many of which were hydrangeas with pink or blue petals.

The island was a veritable paradise in its beauty.

The time was fast approaching when her parents, King Alfredo, and Queen Annelisa, thought Elizabella should consider marrying. But there was a problem, yes, a big problem!

The problem was that Elizabella had been born without arms; yes, without arms!

Unforgettable Sunday Service

By 1st Lt. Joseph Ruff

Excerpt from, *Civil War Experiences of a German Emigrant,* in paperback, ebook, and audiobook, available on Amazon.com and in local stores..

The last Sunday before the battle, a chaplain from an Ohio regiment from Sherman's division, at the request of our chaplain, Eldred, came to hold divine service. The bugle call was announced, and those who were interested, or drawn there, gathered and sat in a circle on the ground. A couple of hardtack boxes had been secured for a pulpit upon which was placed a somewhat dim light. Here, indeed, was a scene for an artist. A familiar hymn or two were sung, after which the chaplain led in prayer. To me this was a very solemn and impressive service and one which I never forgot.

The man of God seemed to be deeply touched, and some high spiritual feeling seemed to inspire him, while a feeling of awe crept over the rest of us. This certainly was in deep contrast to the time, just a week from that very hour, when over some thirty-six-hundred acres of battlefield, thousands of brave men lay silent in death, while numbers, untold, were bleeding and dying, and hundreds of wounded were being moved to the rear. Then the place was to resound with the crack of musketry, the roar of heavy artillery from the gunboats, and mingled groans and shouts of victor and vanquished. What a change from that Sabbath evening's hour of divine service!

Daylight, Day One

Daylight now came streaming through the woods. There was a short lull in the firing, and looking off to the left front, I discovered a cavalry force moving to our left. I called the attention of Major Powell to them and suggested that perhaps they were endeavoring to flank us. He watched them a moment and decided that was what they were trying to do, whereupon he called his bugler and immediately sounded the retreat. As soon as that movement began, the enemy followed, pouring a galling fire upon us. We were endeavoring to carry off our wounded, and so our progress was slow. We had not retreated far when we met Colonel Moore of the 21st Missouri. Infantry with five companies of his regiment. He rated us as cowards for retreating. We warned him not to be too bold, or he would get into trouble. It was not twenty-five minutes after that when he was wounded twice and his force nearly annihilated or put to rout. Major Powell endeavored to hold back the enemy but could not stand against them. Our battle lines gave way, and the Major himself was killed before we reached camp.

Joseph Ruff was born in Obendorf, Germany, March 18, 1841, the oldest of six children. He immigrated to America with his family in 1853 where they settled at Buffalo, NY. Two years later he came to Michigan and found work in Concord, living in the vicinity of Concord and Albion until his death in 1921. During the presidential campaign of 1856 Joseph followed the heated debate over the question of slavery, which often came to blows. He read Uncle Tom's Cabin and the Lincoln/Douglas debates becoming personally convicted on the issue. He proudly voted for President Lincoln, vowing to fight on the side of freedom, serving in the Union Army 1861-1865.

In this stirring memoir, Joseph Ruff recounts his experiences during the first year of his four years of service in Company D of the 12th Michigan Regiment. It was "by far the most severe year of our service, a year of battles, severe marches, constant duties, privations, illness, and death." Beginning as a green new recruit with no fanfare, no uniform and only the bare necessities, Joseph became a seasoned soldier at times living by his wits and off the land. Joseph recounts in harrowing detail his confrontations with the enemy and numerous narrow escapes. There was more than one occasion when Joseph felt that Divine Providence had not only saved him, personally, but had guided the war, as well.

One of the most important battles of the war, the Battle of Shiloh, took place in April 6th of that first year. Joseph writes his account of the experience beginning with a skirmish on the night of April 5th when he and two-hundred soldiers undertook a scouting expedition, little knowing that a force of 42,000 Confederate men was lying in wait prepared to attack next day. Fortunately, Joseph and his squad saw an outlying sentry, saving them from blundering into the entire enemy camp. Even so, they barely escaped through a barrage of bullets and returned to camp.

Thus, they were able to deliver a warning to the Union army, so timely it is thought to have affected the course of the war. Had the Union Army been caught unawares and defeated at Shiloh, it could have handed the Confederacy a victory.

Civil War
Experiences
of a German Emigrant
Company D, 12th Michigan Regiment

"He who cares for all His children must surely have been watching over me."

1st Lt. Joseph Ruff
1841-1921

The book, *Civil War Experiences of a German Emigrant*, by 1st Lt. Joseph Ruff is available in three versions: print, audible and ebook, on Amazon.com, MercerPublications.com and at the Michigan retail establishments listed below:

For Amazon.com go here: (Joseph Ruff Memoirs Series (2 books)

For MercerPublications.com go here: (MercePublications.com MENU):

Or visit these Michigan stores:

Hutch's Food Center, Spring Arbor,

Canadian Lakes Pharmacy, Canadian Lakes

Remes Pharmacy, Remes

Back of the Bookstore, Lakeview]

Chelsea, Michigan 1855"

By 1st Lt. Joseph Ruff (1841-1921)

Excerpt from The Joys and Sorrows of an Emigrant Family

© 2020 Mercer Publications & Ministries, Inc.

Editor's Note: [In his own words, late in life, Joseph Ruff penned his book of memoirs, "The Joys and Sorrows of an Emigrant Family." In this excerpt, he accurately spins an adventure tale of when, as a young man, he traveled "west" to Michigan. The year was 1855. At the age of fourteen, Joseph left his family behind and boarded a "steamer" across Lake Erie from Buffalo, New York, to Detroit, Michigan. Joseph and his new employer, Mr. Whittacre, proceeded across Michigan via horse and carriage to the Whittacre farm near Albion, Michigan. Joseph Ruff's descendants are still in the area. The entire book has recently been republished.]

Chelsea, Michigan 1855

That night we arrived in Chelsea, a quiet little village at that time, now a thriving center. We put up at the only public house, such as you would find in the pioneer days.

One thing I must relate here that always stayed in my memory. As was largely the custom of those days, when there were no telephones or daily papers to bring you the news, the villagers and nearby farmers would drop in and discuss the events of the day. Political, social, and commercial topics were interspersed, often, with stories of what their grandfathers did or some big thing done in New York State, as the majority of the settlers had come from that state.

A Strange New Dance

Not long after supper, there came not only men but young women, and this particular evening they came with violin boxes. I wondered, as a boy would in such a strange place, what was going on. I was not left long in doubt. I heard a cleaning of the dining room furniture going out, and soon the company gathered in the room. The fiddlers tuned up their violins, partners arranged themselves in sets, and all started to the time of the music. They danced to the orders of the caller, such as "balance partners, ladies change, and all promenade," all to the time and rhythm of the music. The music and the exhilaration of the dance, so new and somewhat strange to me, I have never forgotten. One of the dances which struck me as funny was what they called "pop-goes-the-weasel." Mr. Whitacre joined with great pleasure in nearly all the dances.

Grass Lake and Jackson

The next morning we proceeded on our way. It being very hot and sultry, we stopped at Grass Lake, a small village, for rest and dinner, then proceeded on our way through the village of Jackson. As I have often visited Jackson and have done business there, I am always brought back in memory to my first passing through this place and think of the changes since then.

[If you enjoy this excerpt, you can find the book, *The Joys and Sorrows of an Emigrant Family,* by 1st Lt. Joseph Ruff, on Amazon.com, (Joseph Ruff Memoirs Series (2 books) MercerPublications.com, (MercerPublications.com MENU) and at the following Michigan stores:

Hutch's Food Center, Spring Arbor,

Canadian Lakes Pharmacy, Canadian Lakes

Remes Pharmacy, Remes

Back of the Bookstore, Lakeview

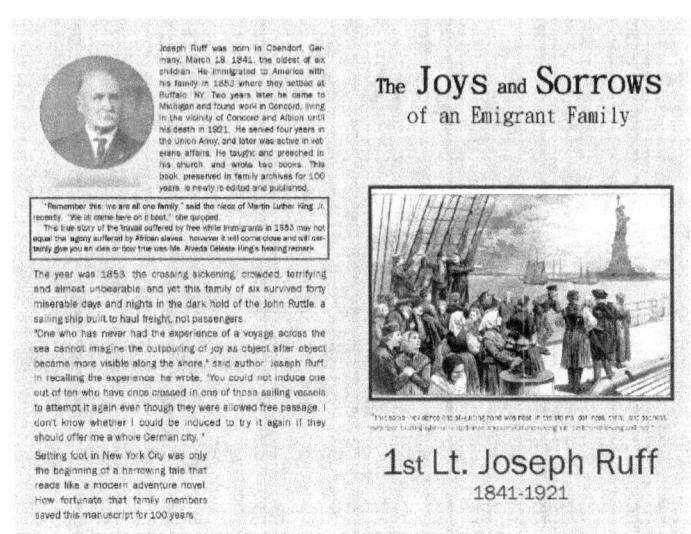

About the Author—1st Lt. Joseph Ruff

Joseph Ruff was born in Obendorf, Germany, March 18, 1841 and departed this life January 19, 1921, aged 79 years, 10 months, and 1 day.

He was the son of Xavier and Catherine Ruff and was the oldest of a family of six children. He immigrated in America with his parents in 1853 and located at Buffalo, New York. Two years later he came to Michigan and settled in Concord and has lived in the vicinity of Albion and Concord ever since.

On December 17, 1861, he enlisted in the Union army at Albion and served four years and two months. He was commissioned First Lieutenant

November 18, 1865, and was mustered out at Camden, Ark., February 15, 1866. He was a member of the local G.A. R. and was commander for four years.

In early manhood he was converted: from Catholicism and united with the Methodist Protestant church and retained this membership until death. He was an active Christian worker and has superintended two Sunday schools at one time. He had also been given a license to preach and conducted services at Concord, Rice Creek and Eckford.

28 Wise Sayings from Beyond the Grave[1]

Recorded by Kevin Hayes

© 2021 K. Hayes

You can never have too many dogs. But you have to clean up after them. So, take that into account.

Be extra nice to the obese and super obese. Go out of your way at social events and have a conversation with them. Prepare yourself for an intelligent discussion. You will likely get one on about any subject.

We all want attention. We all crave positive feedback. Don't expect it for yourself but give it to others anyhow. People will remember that about you.

Learn to be thankful for everything good. Say it out loud. Say it more often than you do.

Don't park in tow-away zones. Get home before midnight.

You have a Guardian Angel who is a messenger from God. Believe me, I know. Listen, and follow your Guardian Angels' voices.

Denying the existence of God does not make you an intellectual. Instead, you will have made yourself into a complete idiot.

----

[1] Recently printed in the Lakeview Area News

Have confidence in yourself, which includes the kind of confidence to be able to laugh at yourself.

Work in jobs you like. Otherwise, you will learn the pay and title of your job won't make you any less miserable, only more stuck.

If you don't have any friends, make friends with those who don't have any friends either. Keep on doing it until you have good friends who have your back and vice-versa.

Teach your children to be good and to be courageous.

If you get sick, make sure your mother is around. Unless your mother is a doctor, then, by all means, call a doctor.

Don't expect things to make you happy. You can't be happy with things. Don't collect junk. Use the stuff you have. Happiness comes from activities, not possessions.

Send cards and letters to the sick and hospitalized, especially to those who are far away.

Addiction is a mystery to me and you, but not to God. When you have tried everything you can think of, try one more thing. Never give up. Avoid judgmentalism. How are you doing with your New Year's resolution? How did that go for each of the last twenty years? What about your own weaknesses?

Did you know you can slow a car down by decelerating and using the brake pedal? I didn't. You don't have to roll it.

Forgive one another as you would wish to be forgiven. Don't waste the short time you have without learning how to let go. Don't sweat the small stuff.

Do the exercise for which your body is made. Don't try to be perfect. Disk golf was one of my favorites, but anything is better than nothing. The point is to do it often enough to become a good habit, and soon you will happily find your body and mind are working together doing something productive instead of just sitting around making up excuses.

Love and stay involved with your family, even including your stepfathers! Fight for them.

I am here watching you. I am in a place—a perfect place—I can't describe. No one wants to die, but don't be afraid of it. There is more to come. Don't worry about that!

Find out seriously just who was and is this person called Jesus Christ. Don't let others do it for you. Find out yourself. Then ponder on why He remains the most ignored, misjudged, and hated person in history. Follow Him. He'll do the rest.

Go Up "North" at least 4...12...365 times a year.

Go to church.

Don't do business with liars. Don't date them either.

Become part of the world of the less fortunate.

Don't carry your cross alone, and help others with theirs when you can.

You will be judged on faith and love. Nothing else is more important in the end. But the end is an eternal beginning.

Thank you for being with me when I was sick and when I died. I was lucky to have you in my life; I proudly carried the family name and always will. Lucky for me, I have made it home and my Guardian Angel has been set free. I will try to help you all from where I am now.

About the Author—Kevin Hayes

Author Kevin Hayes penned these poignant words as part of a eulogy delivered at a memorial service. The deceased woman who departed this earthly coil much too young had failed in her quest to overcome a fatal addiction.

Kevin is a native of Port Huron, Michigan and now resides in St. Johns, MI, with his wife and family. A graduate of Michigan State University and Cooley Law School, he has served as a Rotary International GSE ambassador to India.

Among his other works, Kevin has published two novels, the exciting *Kickland*, about Nordic racing and Olympic glory, and *Don't Vote For Me*, a hilarious account about his running for political office. Both books are available on Amazon.com

When I Was Young

Dorothy May Mercer

When I was young
I thought I might fly,
Life would begin
When I flipped my tassel.

Now I am old
I tell you no lie
Life has become
A significant hassle

When I was young
Thirty-five was ancient
Now that I'm old
Seventy-five was recent

When I was young
Life was for playing
Now that I'm old
What matters is praying.

When I was young
Ice cream was a main dish.
Now that I'm old
For ice cream I now wish.

    When I was young
    No thoughts for the morrow
    Life was a blast
    The die not yet cast.

        Now that I'm old
        Some days spent in sorrow
        Magnificent past
        How long will it last?

Flight 257

By Douglas Maxson

It wasn't unusual for a dense fog to linger at this airstrip. The location provided the right seasonal atmosphere for such a haze. How strange that it positioned above Lindsay's flight without moving!

After her eight years of hard work, Lindsay Monarch, an aspiring author, had landed a major book deal with Vanning Publishing in New York City promising a five-figure advance. She was merely one flight away from stardom, if the thick fog did not ruin her plans.

As she walked to the plane for boarding, a hoodie covered her sandy-colored hair hiding her ponytail. The cool mist hovering around the plane glowed a yellowish gray giving off the smell of sulfur. After Lindsay entered the plane, she shivered from the chill, as if the weird fog and mist had followed her onboard.

While she scanned the rows of seats, a passenger brushed her shoulder with his massive frame. "Hello, Lindsay," he smirked. She returned the gesture focusing her eyes on his rugged face and the deep scar on his right cheek. She hesitated, "Do I know you?"

He stared at Lindsay, forced another sneer, and huffed, "You should!"

As passengers took their seats, Lindsay took one halfway down the aisle near a window with a view of the left wing. As she looked out, the wingtip was obscured because of the thick fog.

A man seated behind her leered. "Like the view? Ha-ha. Just wait. You'll love the flight."

The flight attendant made a final inspection of all passengers while checking their seatbelts. When she reached Lindsay's seat, she simpered, "Nice to see you again, Lindsay."

"W-what are you talking about?" Lindsay's lip quivered.

Lindsay noticed her southern accent and a silver chain around her neck with an angel pendant. The flight attendant, who went by the name Carmella, bent down holding the necklace close to Lindsay. "Like it? You did a nice job with it."

"I don't understand," Lindsay drew away.

A man tapped Lindsay on the shoulder causing her to jump and turn around. "Hi, Lindsay. I'm Frank. I'm not the guy you think I am. When you get to know me, I'm really a nice fellow." He noticed a bag of peanuts resting on Lindsay's lap. He asked, "Are you going to eat those? Cashews are my favorite." He reached over Lindsay's shoulder.

"Hey!" Lindsay nearly shouted. "Is this your idea of nice?" She saw a tattoo of a naked lady on the arm that reached for the peanuts. Though alarmed, it wasn't the image that drew so much attention, it was the caption, 'Rest in Peace, Lindsay.'

Lindsay was about to bolt away when a voice interrupted, from a loudspeaker overhead, "Ladies and gentlemen, this is your captain. In a few minutes we will be taking off. Please make certain your seatbelts are securely fastened and your belongings stowed away in the overhead bin or under the seat in front of you. Enjoy your flight."

The flight attendant made another walk through the row of seats checking passenger's belts. Lindsay pleaded, "Could I please have another seat?"

"What seems to be the problem, Lindsay?"

"It's the creepy guy behind me. He's making me nervous."

Frank overheard the conversation and humored, "She has a thing with men named Frank."

"Please?" Lindsay begged.

"All right. You can have the seat directly across the aisle between those two gentlemen."

"Are you kidding? They better be well-behaved."

"They're well dressed. They look harmless. Much better than what you said about me." Carmella noted.

"What's that supposed to mean?"

"You said the reason I don't have a husband is my taste in clothing is unbecoming."

"I never said that!" Lindsay denied and changed seats, asking, "How long will our flight be to New York?"

The gentleman sitting on her right grinned and said, "Did you hear that people? Lindsay wants to know how long before we land," as he twitched his head uncontrollably.

"Who said anything about landing?" came from the man on her left.

Lindsay tried to ignore the man on her right's unique habits. She turned her head toward the gentleman on her left. "Hi; I'm Lindsay. What's your name?" she offered.

"I'm Detective Alan." He pointed to the other gentleman and said, "Thith is Detective Bower. Perhapth you've heard of uth. We're going to New York to athyth in the trial of Ruby Kelly and Carl Theldon. Ruby ith the one who faked her death for inthuranthe fraud. Both thee and her huthband, Tham, flew to a remote ithland along with their agent, Carl. We located Ruby and Carl in one of the ithland motelth. Tham wathn't ..."

Lindsay interrupted, "They were found floating face down in the ocean. That's in my book, Chapter 12, page 4, paragraph 2. How did you know?"

Detective Alan said, "I thee your familiar with our work. Too bad you were careleth in our thtrange character mannerithms."

"Who are you people?" Lindsay demanded. "I never met you before, and yet I know you. It's obvious you know me. How can that be? Is this some kind of joke?"

"Let's say we are close fans of yours," said the flight attendant.

"There's something strange going on," Lindsay said. This is more than a coincidence."

"Must be." spoke a man from the front.

"And who are you?" asked Lindsay.

"Les. Les Dryson. Hello, Lindsay," he said, as he rolled up his sleeves.

The flight attendant's eyes opened wide. "Nice biceps!" she said.

Lindsay rubbed her sweaty palms together. "They ought to be. I created them. In fact, I created all of you. What's going on here? What do you want?"

Frank said, "Nothing. We've taken care of everything."

"Ladies and gentlemen, this is your captain. Please stay seated. We are now ready for takeoff. Enjoy your flight, Lindsay!"

After the plane lifted off, Lindsay saw the strange fog from the window of the left wing following as if it were attached to the plane.

"Flight 257 is right on schedule," said the flight attendant.

"Flight 257!" Lindsay shouted. "The lady at the airline desk said it was flight 251."

"Oops. Just a slight error." said Carmella.

Lindsay gripped the seat arms until her knuckles turned red. Her chest lifted as she remembered the flight's horrible outcome. "257 never made it to New York!" she cried. "It developed engine trouble and crashed fifteen minutes after takeoff. There were no survivors!"

"Oh, but you're wrong," Carmella disclosed. "All survived, but one."

"That's not the way I ended the book. No survivors."

The plane started to bounce and shake. "Ladies and gentlemen, this is your captain. Please stay seated. We're experiencing some turbulence."

The flight attendant revealed, "It won't be long now. About your book, it will have the ending we all deserve," she exclaimed to cheers and applause. She bent closer to Lindsay's' ear, "It's so sad we have to end it this way, my dear."

Sweat poured off Lindsay's brow. She wiped her face. "You sound like I'm not going to make it to New York. If it's change you want, I can write a different ending," she bargained. "I'll even write nice things about all of you. We don't have to end it this way."

The plane shook causing serving trays and drinks to crash to the floor. Lindsay frantically flipped

178

through her manuscript trying to tear out pages hoping to change the outcome. They welded together making it impossible to remove any pages. Frantically, she leafed to the end, screaming, "What have you done?"

"Like it?" Carmella smirked. "Soon we will get the recognition we deserve. Not the character assassination you created." The passengers clapped hands and laughed with glee.

Lindsay stood and pleaded with her characters. "But you are not real! You are a figment of my imagination! The book can't survive without me." She turned and waved her arms. Tears streaming, she implored, "Please, I beg you. You can't remove the author."

"Oh, but we have," Carmella scoffed. "You're the one who doesn't exist. Flight 257 crashed twenty minutes ago. You would have loved the ending, my dear. Too bad you're going to miss it."

About the Author-Douglas Maxson

My first writing endeavor was over forty years ago entering a writer's contest in our local paper. It was sponsored by Palmer's Writer's School looking for new and upcoming talent. This was the same establishment Peanut's creator Charles Shultz attended.

A little over three years ago, I discovered a writing critique class held in the back room of a Shuler's Bookstore. After visiting a couple of times, I was hooked and ready to pursue the writing career.

Because I was now retired from the construction field, I was able to spend more time studying and honing my craft. My wife said she always knew the gift of writing was in me by the pieces of poetry I left for her on napkins while dating her.

With the help and support of West Michigan Writer's Group, I have successfully published two short stories for The Good Old Day's magazine. I like to write fiction, non-fiction, poetry, and memoirs. I've been working on a children's book and hope to complete it for my next accomplishment.

Because I am still in the infant stage of creative writing, I am always looking for support and guidance of which my critique class and Mercer Publications & Ministries, Inc. has provided me.

I also want to thank my Lord and Savior for stirring up that gift of writing which has always been in me.

The Strongest Man in the World

By Douglas Maxson

As Kong carried his bride across the threshold of their new home, a neighbor across the street shouted, "Hey freaks! Why don't you go back to where you belong like the circus!" With words like that it would have been easy for Kong and Lucy to return to their roots, but they couldn't. They weren't allowed.

Teardrops rolled down Kong's cheek and nestled in Lucy's beard.

As the former "Bearded Lady," she, too, was leaving the traveling show. Tenderly, she wiped the salty tears which tracked the aging lines of Kong's face. Kong (his circus name) knew it wouldn't be easy to leave behind his legacy as "The Strongest Man in the World."

Kong had spent days bringing boxes of their personal things from the circus. But this was the first time his wife, Lucy, saw the new house. He wanted to surprise her but was not expecting this awful welcome from the neighborhood.

Lucy and Kong had spent most of their lives entertaining crowds worldwide. Their oddity was considered to be rather acceptable, never offensive, or freakish, as their new neighbors had shouted.

Lucy started toward the kitchen. Her walk slowed as she made a path between the boxes filled with circus memorabilia. There were pictures and memories of the "Big Top." She couldn't stand the thought of the remains of their circus life being confined to cardboard boxes.

"Kong, dear," she asked, "would you like me to fix you some lunch? All I have is some bread and baloney left over from the circus wagon."

"No, thanks, darling; I'm not hungry. I'll start unpacking some of our stuff." While lifting a box, a framed picture slid off the top. Kong paused as he picked it up. His hands warmed the portrait while a finger traced the faces of his circus family. He slowly walked into the kitchen, his shoulders slumped, as he gazed at that photo.

Lucy shared his warmth as her hand caressed the bulging veins of Kong's hands. "You miss the Big Top don't you? You would still be there if it wasn't for me."

Kong slammed the picture on the kitchen floor. Glass shattered and needled into the surrounding carpet. "Why do you keep saying that?"

"Because it's true, Kong. The circus policy made it clear if any of its employees were to marry other employees, they would be fired."

Kong placed the broken frame and picture on the kitchen counter. He kneeled on the floor. Hands, once used for gripping iron weights, probed the carpet for imbedded glass. A small piece penetrated his calloused hand.

Tears threatened to obscure Lucy's vision as she tried to remove the sliver of glass from Kong's hand. He wiped a droplet from Lucy's cheek with his other hand.

Kong said, "How long did you think I could be the circus strong man? Look at me. That last act nearly did me in. Those five-hundred-pound dumbbells almost tore off my shoulders. Besides, I'm ready for a change, and so are you. This new job and home will be good for us. You'll see."

Lucy stroked her delicate beard. "Maybe for you. But I'm a bigger freak than you are. You heard that neighbor across the street. Who would want to be around a woman with a beard?"

"Don't say that, Lucy! You know I love you and won't let anyone hurt you. Besides, after that appointment with the hormone doctor, that beard you've worn so long will be a thing of the past. Things will be different."

Lucy rubbed her hand across Kong's smooth head. "You really think so?"

"I do, Lucy. Now, cheer up. I think I'm ready for that sandwich."

Suddenly, there was knock at the front door. "Kong, would you, please, see who that is, while I finish making your lunch?"

184

Kong walked to the door and looked through the narrow, glass window. He saw two boys on the porch; one was tinkering with a camera. As soon as he opened the door, the one boy shoved the camera in the pocket of his hooded sweatshirt and started to back away.

The other boy said, "I told you Billy. He's the same guy we saw at the circus. My dad said he saw him with a freak, a woman with a beard."

Meanwhile, Lucy put the sandwich on the table next to Kong's recliner and moved to the front door to see who was there.

When Jimmy, the other boy, saw her join Kong on the front porch, he pushed Billy forward and shouted, "There she is Billy! My dad was right!"

Billie reached into his pocket and pulled out the camera.

"Hurry! Take a picture!" Jimmy urged.

Kong grabbed the camera, ready to slam it on the porch steps. As she wrestled the camera from Kong's hands, Lucy yelled, "No, Kong! They're only kids!" Lucy knew that grip, the one used to wrap his fingers around the circus dumbbells. Her fear for him was greater than the boys' mockery. Kong released his grip. Lucy gave Billie the camera, and both kids ran across the street.

Kong rubbed his hands. "I'm sorry, Lucy. I don't know what came over me." Kong moved back into the house and sagged into the recliner. He finished his sandwich while Lucy did more unpacking. As she was carrying a box from the kitchen into the living room, there was another knock at the door. "Don't answer it," said Kong. "It's probably those pesky kids again."

The pounding became louder, more like someone was kicking the door loose from its hinges. Lucy put the box down, starting toward the door, but Kong stopped her. "Those kids have gone too far, Lucy. Let me handle this."

She grabbed Kong's arm. "Alright but please promise me you won't be too hard on the kids."

He nodded and opened the door. A frantic woman grabbed his arm. "Come quickly! You've got to help my son, Jimmy!" She gestured wildly and pulled. "Hurry, please! He's pinned underneath our car!"

Kong stood firm.

"Over there," she pointed, "across the street!"

The woman's knuckles turned red as she tightened her grip on Kong's arm.

"Wait a minute, lady," Kong protested, "I don't even know you."

Tears rolled down the woman's cheeks. "Please," she begged, "help my Jimmy!"

Lucy's hand met Kong's. "I know it's the same kid, but you have to go. This is a mother's child."

Kong shook his head, "Lucy, it's been a long time since I've lifted anything that heavy, and we're talking about a car weighing over a ton."

"Kong, we're wasting precious time. You can do this."

Kong sighed, "Alright, Lucy. No more talk." Turning toward the frantic woman, he said. "All I can do is try. Show me where he is, Mrs. Hamilton."

She broke into a run, dashing around traffic. Kong followed her across the street and pushed his way through the crowd. Unlike the roar of a circus audience, the moans of a young boy brought a stillness. Other bystanders attempted to lift the car with no success. Fortunately, the full weight of the vehicle was not pressing Jimmy. He could still breathe with some difficulty.

His mother couldn't wait. She grabbed the back bumper, straining to lift that ton of steel, her delicate hands oblivious to the cold sharp metal.

Her husband pried her hands off. Kong stepped in and gripped the back bumper like the bar from those circus dumbbells. He crouched, bending legs like tree trunks, with back and shoulders straight as an oak tree.

A man shouted from the crowd, "Hey loser! I saw your last performance! Pitiful! What makes you think you can lift that car when you couldn't even lift those baby weights!" Another yelled, "Why don't you have your wife do the lifting? She looks more of a man than you do!"

Jimmy's mother said, "Never mind them. Jimmy and I were at the circus. We saw you lift those dumbbells like a sack of potatoes."

Lucy's grin overshadowed her beard. "She's right, Kong. Do it for Jimmy's mother, and the circus."

Kong repositioned his hands, grabbed the bumper like vise-grips, and started to lift. His fingers began to bleed from grasping the sharp edges of the bumper. Beads of sweat formed like raindrops on Kong's head and face. His powerful muscles bulged and quivered.

Lucy wiped the salty streaks blocking his vision. The car creaked as it inched up from Jimmy's chest. Lucy coached Kong. "Keep going! You're almost there!" Others from the crowd shouted, "Go, go. Go Kong go!"

Jimmy's father and others rushed forward to help. When the vehicle cleared Jimmy's chest, they pulled him to safety. Jimmy gasped and complained his chest hurt. When the ambulance finally arrived, the attendants were not expecting Jimmy to be alive. Mr. Hamilton told his wife to ride with Jimmy to the hospital. "I'll catch up as soon as I can," he promised.

Kong was sitting on the concrete driveway. Lucy wiped the blood from his hands and wrapped them in his own discarded shirt. She helped him to his feet.

Mr. Hamilton approached Kong. He extended his hand, but saw his injuries, and instead, put his hand on Kong's shoulder. With the back of his other hand, he wiped a tear of remorse from his face, and said, "Thank you, Kong, for saving our son's life. Leaving that car on blocks was a stupid thing to do, especially when kids play in the driveway. I was wrong about you, and I'm so terribly sorry for making fun of you and your wife. Welcome to the neighborhood."

Kong smiled. "Thank you, Mr. Hamilton."

"Call me Joe."

"Alright, Joe."

Lucy continued to attend Kong's hands. Joe Hamilton approached Lucy. He said, "I've never hugged a woman with a beard before."

Lucy chuckled and raised her arms. "It tickles the same way as a man's beard."

Joe leaned in and said, "You're right. You take care of Kong. I'd better get to the hospital."

Kong inquired, "Mr. Hamilton. Uh, Joe. Do you think I could ride with you to see how Jimmy is doing?"

"Sure, Kong. Jimmy would like that. Better have the doctor look at your hands, too. We never know when we'll need The Strongest Man in the World."

~~~~//~~~~

www.ingramcontent.com/pod-product-compliance
Lightning Source LLC
Chambersburg PA
CBHW061200170626
46809CB00003B/1188

* 9 7 8 1 6 2 3 2 9 0 9 5 5 *